Copyright © 2005 by Robert Vaughan

Publisher: Skyward Publishing, Inc.
             813 Michael Street
             Kennett, Missouri 63857
             E-Mail: info@skywardpublishing.com
             Website: www.skywardpublishing.com

Library of Congress Cataloging-in-Publication Data

Vaughan, Robert, 1937-
   Brandywine's war : "back in country" / Robert Vaughan.
     p. cm.
   ISBN 1-881554-41-4
   1. Vietnamese Conflict, 1961-1975—Fiction. 2.
Americans—Vietnam—Fiction. I. Title.

PS3572.A93B73 2005
813'.54—dc22   2004022921

Second Printing
Printed in the United States of America

Dedicated to

Sam Post

The last lion in a gentleman's profession

Chapter One

"*The Man Who Shot Liberty Valance*," Trapp said.

"Wrong. It's *The Commancheros*," Dagen insisted.

"You're an idiot. How could anyone say that *The Commancheros* is a better picture than *The Man Who Shot Liberty Valance*?"

"Because John Wayne wasn't the star of *The Man Who Shot Liberty Valance*."

"The hell he wasn't," Trapp replied.

"He wasn't the star. Jimmy Stewart was the star. John Wayne gets killed," Dagen said.

"He doesn't get killed; he dies. There's a difference."

"No it isn't. It's the same difference," Dagen said.

Specialist-6 Nathan Trapp and Specialist-5 Boyd Dagen were arguing over which John Wayne movie was the best. Over the last several months they had argued which baseball team was the all-time greatest, the 1946 St. Louis Cardinals or the 1927 Yankees. They had discussed the merits of Coke or Pepsi, Ford or Chevy, Raquel Welch or Sophia Loren, and once they actually came to blows in a spirited discussion whether Captain Marvel could beat Superman in a fight.

"We'll let Mr. Brandywine settle it," Trapp said. "Mr. Brandywine, what do you think is the best movie John Wayne ever made?"

As he contemplated the question, Brandywine rubbed the scar on his upper lip, an old football injury. Although visible, the scar wasn't disfiguring and could almost be said to compliment his six-foot one-inch square frame.

"Oh that's not even close," Brandywine said. "I think his best movie by far, is *The Conqueror.*"

"What?" Trapp and Dagen shouted at the same time.

"Really now, think about it. It has John Wayne, Susan Hayward, Lee Van Cleef. . .great scenery, a sweeping story. . .clearly his best."

"Excuse me, sir. I mean, you being an officer and all, but you don't know shit," Dagen said.

"You got that right," Trapp agreed. "Come on, Dagen. Let's go down to the flight line."

Brandywine watched the two men leave and then stepped into his supply room. He was proud of what he had done to it. It was paneled in pine that had been scorched with a blowtorch to bring out the grain, and then coated with a clear, gleaming varnish. The floor was green and cream tile, while his area, set off by a waist-high wall, was covered with a thick red carpet, courtesy of Miss Song. Two air conditioners hummed efficiently, all products of Brandywine's ingenuity.

Miss Song was posting the property book. She was not only an attractive woman, but she was also efficient and smart, and, to tell the truth, she could have run the supply room without Brandywine or Sergeant Gibson.

Miss Song was Brandywine's Vietnamese secretary and had held the same position for the three men who had been company supply officers before Brandywine. Miss Song had converted to Christianity four years ago, but as she explained to Brandywine, she "didn't want to piss Buddha off," so she didn't totally abandon him. In addition to the cross she wore around her neck, she kept a little statue of Buddha on the corner of her desk.

Gibson, Brandywine's supply sergeant, sat at his desk with his eyelids half closed in a perpetual alcoholic haze. He was working with the forms that seemed to keep him occupied all day.

Staff Sergeant Rodney Gibson was a World War II veteran who had jumped into France with the 101st on D-Day. Of the thirty men in Gibson's platoon, only three had survived the first twenty-four hours.

Gibson had also served in Korea with the Seventh Infantry Division. There he picked up his second

Purple Heart and won the Silver Star for killing seventeen Chinese soldiers when his company bunker was overrun.

Vietnam was his third war and somewhere in between wars he had become an alcoholic. B. Dowling Mudd had criticized Brandywine for carrying Sergeant Gibson, but Brandywine said that on the one or two days a week Gibson was sober, he was better than any other supply sergeant would have been for the entire week.

That wasn't entirely true. Brandywine knew that Sergeant Gibson was trying to go for his full thirty years in order to get a seventy-five rather than a fifty percent retirement pension, and he figured that anyone who had served in three wars had certainly earned that right.

Chief Warrant Officer Three W.W. Brandywine flew helicopters for the 65th Transportation, D.S. Company. Whenever a helicopter crashed either from being shot down or by accident, Brandywine would take a rigging team out to the site and prepare the helicopter for recovery.

But he had also been appointed Supply and Property Book Officer because he could lie, cheat, and steal better than any other officer in the battalion. And it was this, his collateral duty, that provided him with the office he was now occupying.

"You write on your book now, Mister Blandeewine?" Miss Song asked.

"No, I'm doing supply forms."

Miss Song giggled. "I think maybe you write on book but want Major Casey to think you do supply forms."

"I think maybe you know too much," Brandywine said. "I could give you a job working in the back folding sheets and blankets, you know. It's hot back there."

"I don't think you do that," Miss Song said.

Brandywine knew she wasn't really worried about such a thing. She knew that she ran the office. Fortunately, she didn't take advantage of that knowledge, and she and Brandywine actually had a very good working relationship.

"You're right," Brandywine said. He sighed. "I'm just wasting my time anyway. Nobody is going to buy this book."

"I think maybe somebody will. It is very good book."

Brandywine looked at the pile of pages by his typewriter. "Yeah, sure, you like it. But you're just trying to get on my good side," he said.

Brandywine opened his desk drawer and pulled out the latest rejection letter.

Dear Mr. Brandywine:

Thank you very much for submitting for our attention the partial MS of your novel,

Brandywine's War. While the book is amusing, our marketing people tell us that they are unable to sell books with a Vietnam theme. Reluctantly, we must decline, but we wish you luck in placing the book with another house.

Jay Marino, Editor

Brandywine folded the letter and put it in the envelope before putting it back with the seventeen other rejections.

There was another pile of mail in the desk drawer. There were exactly twenty-one letters from his wife. These represented Glenda's schedule of writing to him once every two weeks. He pulled out the most recent one:

Dear WW,

It rained today. I don't like it when it rains, because we have to keep the kids in for recess and they go wild.

I had a salad for lunch today. The cafeteria never makes salads, but there is a refrigerator in the teacher's lounge so I made it before I left home.

Yesterday, I took Sherry to the vet. She had been throwing up and I thought she might be sick, but the vet said I should just

*change her food. I have tried, but as you
know, she doesn't like dog food.*

*There is another teacher whose husband
is in Vietnam, and she was crying yesterday
because there are so many in our school who
are against the war, and they started asking
her how she could stay married to him. I
didn't say anything, because I have not told
anyone you are in Vietnam.*

Glenda

The letters were getting more and more
impersonal, and he had written her a couple of times
commenting on it. He tried to comment with humor
asking in one of his letters if she had gotten his letter
mixed up with one she had meant for her
grandmother. Glenda made no direct response and
in the last twelve letters had even omitted the word
"love," in her closing. At least she didn't end them with
sincerely.

Brandywine had just rolled another sheet of paper
into his typewriter when a shadow fell across his desk.
Looking up, he saw Unsoldier.

"What can I do for you, Unsoldier?" he asked.

"Dude," Unsoldier said, dragging the word out.

"I beg your pardon?"

"Dude," Unsoldier said again. "*The Conqueror.* Far
out Heavy. Bitchin'."

"What the hell are you talking about?"

"Like John Wayne, man. Trapp and Dagen, they said you like *The Conqueror.* You ever watched it high?"

"Uh, no, I'm afraid not."

"Awesome man. Like, you know, take a few tokes, chill out, and watch the Duke." Unsoldier put his fingers to the side of his eyes then pressed them to make them look Oriental. "Bitchin'. Totally bitchin'."

Unsoldier had been in Vietnam for almost three years now, having arrived quite unceremoniously inside a duffel bag.

He had been a student at UC Berkeley, and when the peace movement to which he belonged decided to go to Travis Air Force Base to picket the military who were leaving for Vietnam, he went with them.

Unsoldier hoped to find one GI who would desert and whose cause the movement could champion. He entered into a conversation with a group of soldiers his own age. He was carrying a sign which read "Peace Now," but the gentle message didn't help him. He was dropped to his knees by a neat right cross to the chin from a disgruntled Spec-4 from Foley, Alabama.

"Why don't we see how the son of a bitch likes it over there?" someone yelled. Another dumped the contents of one of the duffel bags, and they stuffed Unsoldier inside.

When they arrived in Vietnam eighteen hours later, Unsoldier was tired, hungry, frightened and decidedly less militant.

He walked through the terminal, a sea of military

men stiffly starched and ramrod tall in stateside khakis. He fell in behind a group of newly-arrived GIs and followed them out of the terminal. When they climbed into one of the trucks, he climbed in with them, sitting quietly in the back, conscious of the stares and the curious whisperings going on among his fellow passengers.

When the truck reached the Replacement Company, someone grabbed him, and he found himself standing in front of a man who identified himself as the company commander.

"You are a disgrace to your uniform," the captain said. "Sergeant," he said to the NCO who stood near him. "This man is a disgrace to his uniform."

"I don't have a uniform, man," Unsoldier answered.

"Don't you dispute the captain, soldier," the sergeant said, gruffly. "If he says you are a disgrace to the uniform, then you are a disgrace to your uniform, even if you don't have one."

"If you say so, man," Unsoldier answered.

"Guys like this son of a bitch give me a pain in the ass," the sergeant said. "In the brown shoe army we knew how to handle wiseass punks like this. This new modern Army with the young punk-ass kids, they don't even know how to sojer, by God."

"I'm not a soldier," Unsoldier said.

"Look at you," the captain said. "You call yourself a soldier?"

"No."

"Punk-ass kid don't even no how to say 'sir' to a captain," the sergeant said. "He ain't no sojer."

"I ought to take action to have you boarded out of the Army," the captain said.

"I'm not in the Army," Unsoldier answered.

"Busting you down to private is not enough," the captain said. "I think I'll bust you all the way to the rank of Unsoldier."

"Unsoldier?"

"From now on until such time as you receive orders returning you to the States, you will be addressed as Unsoldier."

"When will I get those orders?" Unsoldier asked.

"Don't worry, D.A. won't forget you. We all get orders eventually."

"Yeah," the sergeant said. "The Army takes care of its own."

The captain and the sergeant were partially correct. They both received orders sending them back home. So did everyone else in the unit. Everyone except Unsoldier, who became a fixture in the company area. He was issued uniforms and fed in the mess hall. He was allowed to sleep in the barracks, but he was faced with two problems. One was that without orders assigning him and from which his return date could be computed, orders could never be cut sending him back home.

His other problem was money. Unsoldier never received pay. A finance clerk who hated loose ends did process a pay voucher for him. Once a month Unsoldier was forced to move through a long pay line to pick up a voucher with the total due of exactly $000.00.

Chapter Two

"Hey, Chief, we've got a recovery near Tay Ninh," Trapp said, sticking his head through the door.

"Damn, I haven't had lunch," Brandywine said. He pulled out a dollar in script, the military pay certificates that passed as money for the GIs in Vietnam, and handed it to Trapp. "Get me a hamburger, French fries, and a Coke, would you? I'll help Dagen and Hanlon get the gear loaded. Have you told B. Dowling Mudd yet?"

"I think he's at lunch now," Trapp said. "I'll let him know."

As Trapp left, Brandywine opened the bottom right drawer of his desk and pulled out a felt bag that looked as if it might contain a bowling ball. What the bag held was a "Helmet, aviation protection, APH-5."

"Unsoldier, I'd love to discuss the Duke with you, but I've gotta run."

"S'okay, Dude," Unsoldier said. "Like, you cats are over here saving the world, know what I mean? When Johnny comes marching home, don't sit under the apple tree, over there, all that shit. Once I was blind, but now I see."

"Right," Brandywine said hurrying from the supply room even as Unsoldier hurled other accolades toward him.

"Thirty seconds over Tokyo, Li'l Marlene, the white cliffs of Dover, America the Beautiful, Kate Smith, Babe Ruth...."

Mercifully, his voice faded as Brandywine hurried toward the flight line.

He hoped Trapp could find B. Dowling Mudd. If not, Brandywine might have to fly with Captain Martin or Captain Hicks or even, God forbid, Captain Fender.

Chief Warrant Officer Three B. Dowling Mudd was not only the best pilot in the company, he was also Brandywine's best friend. B. Dowling Mudd was absolutely convinced of the righteousness of the war in Vietnam and of the American way. He religiously followed baseball, though in truth he didn't like baseball; he claimed that apple pie was his favorite dessert, even though it gave him heartburn, and he could quote entire passages of the FM 22-5, the Army Field Manual for Dismounted Drill and Ceremonies.

Brandywine was fascinated by B. Dowling Mudd because the latter represented everything about the Army that Brandywine didn't like. The two officers had met in flight school, served together in Germany, and now were together again in Vietnam. B. Dowling Mudd was the Production Control Officer, in addition to being, like Brandywine, a recovery officer.

The nose of the UH-1D was decorated with the patch of the 65th Trans, and the logo: "You crash and call . . . we dash and haul." With Dagen standing fireguard, Brandywine started the engine as soon as he saw the jeep arriving with Trapp and B. Dowling Mudd. He was gratified to see that Trapp had brought his lunch.

As soon as all were on board, Brandywine beeped it up to 6600 RP and then pulled pitch.

"Capital Control, Good Nature Three at the 65th Maintenance Hanger, ready for take off," B. Dowling Mudd said.

"Good Nature Three, altimeter two niner, niner, seven, winds north, northeast at five knots, cleared for departure over antennae farm."

"Good Nature Three."

The flight to Tay Ninh was quick and uneventful. The helicopter they were going to recover had gone down earlier in the day, not from enemy action, but from mechanical malfunction. As a result, it was in one piece, sitting in a rice field, and easily visible. Brandywine circled once and set up his approach, landing no more than thirty yards away. He killed the engine then, and as the blades spun down, a lieutenant came toward them. The lieutenant's face was sunburned, his clothes were dirty, and it was obvious that he and his platoon had been in the field for several days.

"I'm providing you with security," the lieutenant said. "How long will this take? My guys have been out for two weeks. We were all ready to go back when this damn thing went down this morning."

"It doesn't look hard. I think we can have it ready in about fifteen minutes. Then all we have to do is wait for a Chinook to come pull it out."

"You don't do that?"

Brandywine shook his head. "Can't do it with this helicopter. All I do is have the guys get it ready. Any bad guys around?"

"Not that we've seen."

Brandywine walked with Trapp and the rigging crew to look at the downed bird.

"Looks like it had a clean autorotation, Chief," Trapp said. "All we need is a lifting eye."

Brandywine nodded. "Okay, get started."

While Trapp, Dagen, and Hanlon started rigging, Brandywine walked back to the helicopter and sat in the open cargo door with his legs hanging out. He grabbed the sack from the PX, pulling out the hamburger and French fries. Sticking a few of the fries in his mouth, he began unwrapping the hamburger.

"Brandywine," B. Dowling Mudd said.

"What?"

"Look."

B. Dowling Mudd nodded toward the men in the security platoon. Like their lieutenant, all were grubby, sunburned, and worn. And all were staring at Brandywine with hungry, envious eyes. One of the men was eating from a can of C-rations and seeing the hamburger, he looked into his can, then tossed it away in disgust.

"Damn," Brandywine said, to B. Dowling Mudd. "I guess I'm the asshole of the hour, huh?"

He took another bite of his hamburger as he glanced down at his flight suit. It was fresh and clean, the result of the hooch girls who did the laundry every day.

Suddenly, there was the sound of several rounds being fired, and tossing his hamburger and French fries, Brandywine leaped down from the helicopter, belly flopping into the mud of the rice paddy.

"Sorry," one of the soldiers said. "I thought I saw something."

"I know what you were doing, Taylor," the lieutenant said. "And if you do it again, I'll have your ass."

"Yes, sir," Taylor said, contritely.

Brandywine looked up from his prone position and saw that the security platoon had formed a semicircle around him.

"Sorry 'bout your lunch, sir," one of them said. He held out an unopened can of C rations. "Want some ham'n eggs?"

"Uh, no," Brandywine said as he stood up and looked down at his mud-stained uniform. "I think I've had enough." He started toward the helicopter, then stopped and turned back toward the men. "But I know one damned thing. Next time I bring a hamburger and French fries into the field I'm going to bring enough for everybody."

Taylor laughed. "You're all right, sir," he said. "Hell, now you even make me sorry I did that."

"Yeah, I'm sure you are," Brandywine said.

"Chief," Trapp called. "Get a shithook in here. We're ready."

Brandywine put on his flight helmet, then keyed the mike.

"Any Hillclimber, any Boxcar, this is Good Nature Three, over."

"Good Nature Three, this is Hillclimber Fifty-one. Where are you?"

"About fifteen clicks east of Tay Ninh. Can you respond?"

"I'll be there in ten minutes. Hillclimber Fifty-one."

Ten minutes later, as promised, the large twin

rotor CH-47 approached. Brandywine pulled the pin on a smoke grenade and tossed it into the field. This served two purposes: it located them, and it gave the Chinook pilot his wind direction.

"Good Nature, I see yellow."

"Roger yellow."

The Chinook made its approach and hovered over the top of the downed helicopter. Trapp, fighting the hurricanic downwash of the twin rotor blades, stood on the transmission deck reaching up until he was able to grab hold of the sling cable and hook. Dagen stood out front giving arm signals to the pilot.

Trapp made the connection and jumped down and ran out of the way. Dagen signaled that the connection was made, and the pilot started his lift.

The helicopter was pulled up from the rice paddy, dripping mud and water as it was jerked free. The Chinook lifted it straight up for several feet, then turning, started back toward Tan San Nhut.

"Let's go!" Brandywine called. "Lieutenant, thanks!"

"You got it, Chief."

With his crew recovered, Brandywine lifted off and started back.

"Hey, Chief, what happened back there? Did you lose your lunch?" Trapp asked, over the intercom.

"Yeah."

"If you don't mind my saying so, it serves you right."

"Why Trapp, when did you become so sensitive to others' feelings?" Brandywine asked.

"Hell, Chief, I ain't talkin' 'bout their feelings. I don't give a rat's ass about the grunts' feelings. I mean, it serves you right because you think *The Conqueror* is the Duke's best movie."

"Damn straight," Dagen agreed. "It serves you right."

When Brandywine returned to the supply room, he put his APH-5 in the bottom right drawer of his desk. Then he went into the back, stripped out of his muddy flight suit, and put on a clean one.

It wasn't until he came back to his desk that he saw it: a buff-colored envelope with dark blue print for the return address.

PENDARROW HOUSE PUBLISHERS
415 CENTRAL PARK WEST
NEW YORK, NEW YORK, 10025

"Miss Song, what is this?" he asked, holding up the envelope.

"It come for you in mail call," Miss Song said.

"Is this all? Just this envelope? Didn't I get my manuscript back?"

"Just letter."

Brandywine stared at the envelope for a long moment, too frightened to open it. This was different from all the others. Every other rejection letter had been included in the return of the self-addressed and self-stamped envelope that he had sent with his submission.

And getting stamps had not been that easy, since all mail from Vietnam was franked. Breathing a quick prayer and taking a deep breath, Brandywine opened the envelope. Within the first few lines, he felt his head spinning, his stomach churning, and his knees weak.

Dear Mr. Brandywine:

> *It is with pleasure that we are prepared to offer you a contract for your delightful novel, Brandywine's War. We propose to pay you an advance of fifteen thousand dollars for hardback rights. We further propose to retain fifty percent of paperback rights, for which we have found a publisher.*
>
> *In your cover letter, you stated that you would be back in the United States by January 19th. We can sell the paperback rights to Foster Crescent House, but in order to do so, the publisher wants to meet you in person.*
>
> *However, Ralph Day is going abroad for an extended stay on the 12th, and he wants to have next season's publishing schedule in place before he leaves. Would it be possible for you to meet with us in New York on the 9th of January?*
>
> *I cannot overemphasize the importance of this meeting, Mr. Brandywine. The*

entire deal, to include our hardback offer,
may well rest upon the outcome.

Sincerely,
Sam Silverman

"Ahh!!!" Brandywine shouted, standing up so quickly that his chair fell over with a loud pop.

"Mister Blandeewine, you okay?" Miss Song asked in concern.

Brandywine was holding his letter out in front of him, staring at it as if in shock.

"I sold my book," he said. "I sold my book! I SOLD MY BOOK!!" he shouted at the top of his lungs.

Chapter Three

CW-3 Walter Winchell Brandywine, W2123490, MOS 671A, had served nearly a full year in Vietnam on what was now his second tour in country. He knew that many people were routinely getting up to forty-five day early drops, so he was absolutely positive that he would be able to get home fifteen days early. That would give him plenty of time to get to New York for the meeting.

In fact, Brandywine was so convinced of this that he wrote to Sam Silverman accepting the offer and promising to be in New York in time for the meeting.

But Lieutenant-Colonel Emile Cleaver, the battalion commander, had other plans. Despite the fact that Major Casey had approved Brandywine's request for an early drop, Cleaver turned it down. He told Brandywine he could go home to sign the contract only if he would take a thirty day leave and agree to come back to Vietnam to serve six more months.

"Would you be willing to do that?" Cleaver asked.

"Colonel, everybody is getting early drops now."

"Yes, but they are by chance, not by selection. If you would like to take a chance on getting an early drop, then there is no need for this conversation."

Brandywine shook his head. "I can't do it by chance. I have to be there."

"The only way you are going to do that is by taking a leave because I will not approve a fifteen day early drop."

In frustration, Brandywine ran his hand through his hair. He sighed, audibly. "All right, Colonel," he said. "If the only way I can be certain to get to New York in time is take a leave and a six month extension, I'll do it."

"I thought you might see it my way," Colonel Cleaver said with a victorious smile. "Oh, and your leave will be chargeable."

"My leave is chargeable? Wait a minute, Colonel, whenever someone extends for six months, they are given uncharged leave."

"You aren't voluntarily extending," Cleaver replied. "You are extending only because it is important for you to be in the States on a certain date. It is important, isn't it? I mean, that is what you have been telling me."

"Yes, sir, it is extremely important."

"In that case, you also won't mind paying your own way to the States and back to Vietnam," Colonel Cleaver said.

"Wait a minute. Not only is my leave chargeable against accrued leave time . . . you are now telling me I have to pay my own way?"

"That's right."

"That's a lot of money," Brandywine complained.

"What do you care?" Cleaver asked. "You're a big time author now. You can afford it. Now that is the deal, Mr. Brandywine. And you can either take it or leave it."

"I'll take it," Brandywine said with a frustrated sigh.

Brandywine and B. Dowling Mudd were having dinner at the Red Bull, the officers open mess on Cong Ly. The Red Bull was shared by the 365th Aviation Battalion, of which the 65th was a part, and the Third Field Hospital. Brandywine was eating a steak with an egg and a side of French fries. He always ate an egg with his meals because he hated eggs, and he had the idea that if he contaminated his food with eggs, he wouldn't eat as much.

His theory didn't seem to be working, and he spent a lot of time trying to avoid the flight surgeon. He was afraid the flight surgeon might put him on the scales, and if so, Brandywine would be grounded for being overweight.

"He is an asshole," Brandywine said, making a face as he took a bite of the egg and steak.

"He is our battalion commander," B. Dowling Mudd said.

"Yes, and our battalion commander is an asshole."

"Even if you think such a thing, you shouldn't say it out loud," B. Dowling Mudd said. "What if someone heard you?"

"Hell, I wanted you to hear me."

"Not me. What if someone heard you and it got back to Colonel Cleaver?"

"Well, it wouldn't be new information, would it? I mean, don't you think he already knows that he is an asshole?"

"Shhh," B. Dowling Mudd said, putting his finger to his lips. "Ever since I have known you, you have put your career in jeopardy with your intemperate action."

Brandywine laughed. "Intemperate action," he said. "I like that. I might use that some time."

"You know what I mean. If getting back to New York by January ninth is that important to you, then you have no choice but to take the Colonel's offer."

"Oh, I'm taking him up on his offer, all right. Only I'm not paying my own way back to the States."

"How are you going to get around it?"

"This way," Brandywine said, handing him a mimeographed sheet of paper.

"What is this?" B. Dowling Mudd asked.

"It's an extract from my orders as a courier. By acting as a courier, my trip back to the States is paid for."

"Does Colonel Cleaver know about this?"

"No, and what he doesn't know won't hurt him," Brandywine said.

"You are always just on the edge of getting yourself into serious trouble, Brandywine."

"I like to walk on the edge," Brandywine said.

"I know. That's why I worry about you."

"Gee thanks, Mom," Brandywine teased.

B. Dowling Mudd continued to examine the papers for a moment. He frowned and shook his head. "No, wait a minute. This won't work," he said, handing the orders back.

"What do you mean . . . it won't work? Of course it will work."

"No, it won't." B. Dowling Mudd pointed to the paragraph extract. "Look, right here. Your flight leaves at ten hundred hours tomorrow morning."

"That's right," Brandywine said.

"Your leave doesn't begin until the next day. Colonel Cleaver won't let you go a day early."

"I won't ask him."

B. Dowling Mudd's eyes grew large. "Brandywine, you can't do that. Technically, you would be AWOL."

"No, I wouldn't. Once I get on this plane, I will be in compliance with these orders, so I can't be charged with AWOL. The courier orders don't expire until I reach CONUS, and by the time I get there, I will then officially be on leave."

"How are you going to get away? Colonel Cleaver is coming down to meet with all the officers of the 65th at o-nine-hundred tomorrow morning. He wants to talk about our readiness reports."

"I've taken that into account," Brandywine said. "I'm already packed, and I'm going to take my gear over to the terminal early in the morning. I'll show up for Colonel Cleaver's meeting, but I'm going to find some way to leave."

"It'll never work," B. Dowling Mudd said.

"Why not?"

"Well, for one thing, your leave won't start until you sign out. If you are in San Francisco, how are you going to sign out?"

"I've got that covered," Brandywine insisted.

"How?"

"Miss Song is going to sign out for me."

B. Dowling Mudd had just taken a swallow of iced tea, and he almost choked on it.

"Miss Song? You are going to let an indigenous female sign you out?"

"Yep."

"What in the world makes you think you can get away with something like that?"

"There's nothing to it," Brandywine said. "Miss Song can sign my name just like I do. Hell, she already signs the readiness reports for me."

"What?" B. Dowling Mudd glanced nervously around the club, and in a quiet voice he leaned across the table saying, "Don't you realize that those readiness reports are classified?"

"Yeah, I know that. But Cleaver makes us juice'em up to look better anyway, so classified or not they are false. I won't sign a false document, so Miss Song signs them for me."

B. Dowling Mudd shook his head slowly. "You are incorrigible," he said.

"Yeah, well sometimes it pays to be incorrigible, doesn't it? If I hadn't figured out some way to trade your medal of honor for a get-out-of-jail-free card, you would be in Fort Leavenworth, right now."

B. Dowling Mudd's face reddened. "That's true," he admitted ignominiously.

Before transferring to the 65th, B. Dowling Mudd had been a gunship pilot for the 86th Helicopter Assault Company, always volunteering for the most dangerous missions. That had earned him a recommendation for the Medal of Honor, but in a bit of Machiavellian manipulation, a general who wanted to be known as the "Peace" general, changed the orders.

Instead of being awarded the Medal of Honor, B. Dowling Mudd was court-martialed and found guilty for the murder of the enemy soldiers he had killed in the action.

It was only by Brandywine's manipulations, getting the Medal of Honor transferred to General Deegle that he was able to get the results of B. Dowling Mudd's court-martial overturned.

In that same operation, he also managed to get the general arrested and the Medal of Honor rescinded.

Brandywine checked his watch. It was about a quarter till nine and the officers of the 65th were gathered in the Wet Mouse waiting for Colonel Cleaver to arrive.

The Wet Mouse was officially the 65th Officers' Lounge. Some of the more ambitious officers of the first deployment had constructed the lounge between two officers' hooches. A roof had been stretched between the two buildings, a floor laid, and walls built at either end. Two air-conditioners and three refrigerators, well stocked with beer, helped the officers fight the heat. One wall was pine paneled and a red leather bar curved around the corner. The wall was decorated with artifacts of the war: a tail rotor, bent and twisted out of shape, a VC flag, a Chinese AK-47 rifle, and an unrecognizable piece of leathery material bearing the unlikely legend of "Ho Chi Minh's Penis."

It was these same officers who had given the

lounge its name. According to the story that had been passed down from officer to officer and tour to tour, shortly after the lounge was built, a mouse had fallen into a glass of beer. The mouse didn't drown because it drank its way to safety, but they found it the next morning, soaked with beer and passed out drunk on the floor. The mouse was long gone, dead, or AWOL, but the lounge was still referred to as the Wet Mouse.

Major Casey, who was commanding officer of the 65th, sat at a table in the back of the lounge carefully stripping the foil from chewing gum wrappers. Captain Fender, the XO, was sniffing on his inhaler. Captain Martin, OIC of the Aviation Depot Open Storage was doing a cat in the cradle with a looped piece of string. Captain Hicks, OIC of the Aviation Depot Warehouse Storage, sat looking at a *Playboy Magazine* holding it sideways in order to study the centerfold.

B. Dowling Mudd was sitting erect, somewhat apart from the others with his hands folded on the table in front of him. Brandywine was leaning against the wall, chewing on a rubber band, and keeping a close eye on his watch. He was a little nervous about whether or not Cleaver would arrive in time. In order for his plan to work, it was important that Cleaver see that he was present when the meeting started.

Cleaver's staff car stopped out front and a moment later the short, bald, and rather stocky lieutenant colonel came into the lounge.

"Tenhut! Sniff!" Captain Fender said, punctuating his call with a loud sniff on his inhaler.

"As you were, gentlemen, as you were," Cleaver replied. He looked over at Brandywine. "Well, Mr. Brandywine, unless I miss my guess, it is getting close to the time you take your leave of us."

"Yes, sir," Brandywine said. "Tomorrow."

"Your *temporary* leave of us, I should say," Cleaver added with an evil chuckle. "I sure hope you get a good deal on your . . . *book contract.*" Cleaver set the words apart from the rest of the sentence in a clear indication that he didn't believe there was such a thing. "I mean, after all, something has to be worth your coming back for six more months."

"Yes, sir, I hope I get a good deal too," Brandywine said. "Oh, by the way, I paid Miss Song to bake a cake for me. It has the title of my book on the icing, and I thought as sort of a celebration of the book, I'd bring it in here. We could have cake and coffee during our meeting."

"Well, Brandywine, that's damn considerate of you," Cleaver said. "Yes, a little cake would go down easy right now. I didn't eat breakfast this morning."

"I'll go get it," Brandywine said. "There's no need for me to be here for the meeting. Captain Fender has already cleared the property book for me. Right, Captain?"

"Sniff, snit," Captain Fender replied with an affirmative nod of his head.

"Very well, Mister Brandywine, go get the cake," Cleaver said.

B. Dowling Mudd looked up in disapproval. He nodded a warning toward Brandywine, but it was obvious from the smile on Brandywine's face and the twinkle in his eyes that he wasn't going to pay any attention to his friend's urge toward caution.

"Oh, Mr. Brandywine, I get a corner piece," Cleaver said. "I like the extra icing. And the good thing about being a colonel is I can get my way on little things like this."

Cleaver laughed, and obsequiously, the others laughed with him.

"Yes, sir, I'll see to it that you get a corner piece," Brandywine said as he left the Wet Mouse.

Ten minutes later Brandywine had checked his baggage through and was now standing in the terminal getting the courier's attaché case handcuffed to his wrist. A Pan Am 707 sat in front of the terminal ready to be boarded for the trip home.

"Are you asking us to fudge the readiness reports, Colonel?" Captain Martin asked.

"No, no, nothing like that. It's just that of late I've been taking a lot of static from . . ." Colonel Cleaver's words were drowned out by the roar of a departing airliner.

"There goes another freedom bird on its way

home," Captain Martin said. "Forty-two days and a wake-up and that'll be me."

Cleaver waited until the sound of the engines receded. "I wonder what's keeping Brandywine with that cake," he asked. He rubbed his stomach. "I'm getting hungry."

Chapter Four

When the airplane touched down at Travis Air Force Base, a cheer went up from the passengers who were soldiers returning from a year's tour of duty in Vietnam. Because he was a courier, Brandywine was sitting in the right front seat of the airplane. He was wearing a pistol on his belt, and the attaché case was handcuffed to his left wrist.

As they taxied toward the terminal building, Brandywine looked through the window, enjoying his first glimpse of the continental USA in nearly a year. He saw the ground guide wearing a bright orange vest and protective ear coverings. He was holding up lighted batons to direct the pilot into the aircraft's parking spot. He also saw what appeared to be a small crowd just on the other side of the perimeter fence.

The stewardess came to his seat and leaned over him. The juxtaposed positions afforded him an excellent view of a rather generous cleavage and shamelessly he partook of the opportunity

The stewardess smiled.

"Mister Brandywine?"

"Yes?" Brandywine continued to stare.

"I'm up here," she said.

"Oh, yes," Brandywine said, looking into her face then. Her face was pretty too, he decided. "I was just, uh, well, I was just…"

"I know what you were just," she said, "and let's say I appreciate being appreciated. But I wanted to tell you that since you are a courier, you will be the first one off the airplane. You can come with me now."

"Thanks.

Brandywine followed her to the front door and stood there until someone tapped on the outside. The stewardess turned the handle and pulled the door open. The air stair was drawn up to the plane.

"Buh, bye," she said.

"Buh, bye. I've always wondered. Do you actually learn to say that in stewardess school?"

"Yes, but not until the last week," she replied. "That's part of our advanced studies."

Laughing at her good sense of humor, Brandywine stepped off the plane, then sniffed the California air: a blend of flowers, sea, and in this case, jet fuel. At the foot of the air stairs, an Army captain and a sergeant were waiting.

He went down the steps to them.

"Are you looking for this?" he asked, lifting the attaché case.

"Yes, let me see your courier orders and ID, please," the captain said.

Brandywine produced both documents.

The captain examined them and then began signing a receipt while at the same time the sergeant unlocked the handcuffs.

"I'm finished with this now, right?"

"Right," the captain said handing the receipt to Brandywine. "But you'll need to keep this for seven years."

Brandywine laughed. "Seven years? What the hell was I carrying, atomic bomb secrets or something?"

"We never know," the captain admitted.

By now the rest of the airplane was emptying, and Brandywine followed the crowd into the terminal building. Once inside, he balled up the receipt and tossed it into the nearest trashcan.

After passing through the terminal, the returning soldiers were directed to a line of dark blue busses marked with U.S. Air Force markings. Airmen on the sidewalks indicated that it didn't make any difference which bus they chose. All would take them to the San Francisco Airport where they would catch flights to their various destinations. Boarding one of the busses, Brandywine settled down about three seats back from the driver. He noticed, with some curiosity, that on the outside all the windows were covered with a very heavy-gauge wire mesh.

"Hey, man," one of the soldiers asked. "What's with this chicken wire?"

"You'll see," the driver replied without further explanation.

Once the bus was filled, the driver closed the door then started the engine. They drove away from the terminal and passed the hangars where several airplanes could be seen parked on the tarmac, some bracketed by yellow maintenance stands. Pulling away from the flight line, they passed through the gate as an Air Police guard waved them through.

"Kerwhump!!"

It sounded like something struck the outside of the bus just below where Brandywine was sitting. Startled, he looked through the window to see what it was.

About twenty young men, most of them wearing long hair, beards, and beads, were standing on the side of the road. As the bus passed by, these same young men began throwing bricks, large rocks, and bottles at the bus. The missiles were hitting the bus, particularly the wire-mesh screens over the windows. As the bottles hit, they would burst. He could see then the reason for the wire mesh.

"Incoming!" someone shouted diving for the aisle.

A few laughed nervously at the young man who but thirty-six hours earlier had been crawling around on the jungle floor.

"What the hell?"

"What's going on?"

"Keep all the windows closed!" the driver shouted. "Keep the windows closed and nobody will be hurt."

"Baby killers!"

"Pigs!"

"Nazi bastards!" those outside screamed at the bus as the driver accelerated on through the gauntlet.

After another few seconds, the missiles stopped and the bus continued the rest of the trip without further incident.

"Damn, do they do that to every bus?" a soldier right behind the driver asked.

"Yes," the driver answered. "Even to the busses marked with red crosses."

For the rest of the trip, a subdued tone replaced the excited buzz of conversation that had been on everyone's lips when they boarded.

The attacks in the San Francisco Airport Terminal were not physical, though Brandywine noticed that the expressions in the faces of many who saw him were anything but supportive.

At the ticket counter, Brandywine bought a ticket to Newport News, Virginia, with an arrival time of seven o'clock the next morning. He went into one of the telephone booths and called home reversing the charges.

"Hello," he heard Glenda's voice say.

"I have a long distance telephone call from W.W. Brandywine. Will you accept the charges?"

"Where is he calling from?"

"Where am I calling from? What difference . . ."

"Sir," the operator interrupted. "I will have to cut you off." Then, to Glenda, she said. "The call is originating from San Francisco."

"I'll accept the charges."

"Go ahead, sir."

"What do you mean, where was I calling from?"

"If you were calling from Vietnam, I didn't want to have to pay for it. Why, there's no telling how much that would cost."

"I'm not in Vietnam; I'm in San Francisco."

"Yes, that's what the operator said."

"Well, don't you think that calls for a little more enthusiasm?" he asked. "I'm back home. Well, in San Francisco, anyway."

"That's good."

Brandywine had almost forgotten how totally devoid of any emotion Glenda could make her voice. They had met and married in Germany where Glenda had been a schoolteacher for the dependant children of the U.S. Army.

Glenda had never been a very demonstrative woman, even in the beginning. But after seven years of marriage, including his tour in Vietnam, she had become even more distant, as evidenced by the almost form letters she had sent him every other week while he was in country.

"Yes, well, I get in to Newport News tomorrow morning at o-seven-hundred. How about picking me up then?"

"Tomorrow is Saturday," Glenda said.

"So?"

"I sleep in on Saturdays. Why don't you take a cab?"

"A cab," Brandywine said. He sighed. "Yeah, you sleep in, Glenda. I'll get a cab."

Ticket in hand, Brandywine was waiting in the lounge when a young boy of about seven came up to him.

"Are you a real Army man?" the boy asked.

"Yes, siree," Brandywine replied, smiling at the boy. The boy smiled back and raised his left hand to salute.

"No, no, you always salute with your right hand," Brandywine corrected. "And hold your hand and fingers straight . . . like this." Brandywine took the boy's right hand and put it over his right eye, then began correcting the salute.

"Timmy!" the boy's mother said. "Get back over here."

"Oh, he's not bothering me, ma'am," Brandywine said.

"I'm not concerned about him bothering you," the woman said with venom dripping from her voice. "I just don't want my son around anyone who would wear that . . . that disgusting uniform."

"I'll just get out of your way then," Brandywine said.

Brandywine began strolling through the terminal trying to pass the time until his flight left. Before long, he was approached by two young men and a young woman. All three were wearing saffron robes, and all three were festooned with beads and flowers in their hair. One of them held out a tract.

"Peace, brother. Let us talk to you about the salvation of your soul," the one with the tract said.

"Oh, thank you, God, you have sent me three more sinners to save!" Brandywine suddenly shouted assuming the tone of a tent evangelist. He clasped his hands together in prayer. "Jay-sus-a. Come into the hearts of these poor lost souls: two brothers and a sister."

"Read this tract," one of the cultists said. "Read, so that you may be enlightened about our leader, Brother Michael."

"Oh, this is worse than I thought," Brandywine said. "Brothers and sister, get down on your knees!" he demanded, pointing to the floor. "Get down on your knees, now, and pray with me. We've much work to do if I am to get that false prophet from your hearts."

"Uh, Brother Michael is . . ." the young woman started.

"Open up their hearts. Heal them of their sins and inequities!" Brandywine shouted, really getting into the rhythm now. He held his hands out over them. "Lord, I pray that you give me the strength to pray non-stop, the twenty-four hours it will take to save these poor, lost souls."

The three cultists looked at each other for a brief moment with an expression of total confusion on their faces. Then, quickly, they started walking away.

"No, my brothers and sister, no!" Brandywine called after them. "Don't leave! Stay with me! There is much work to be done!"

Their rapid walk turned into a run, and those near enough to see what had happened began laughing. A few even applauded, and Brandywine thanked them with a sweeping bow.

It was about a quarter till eight the next morning when Brandywine paid the taxi driver, then walked up to the front door of his house. There was a sign on the door.

The key is where we used to leave it. Don't wake me. G.

"So much for the welcome home," Brandywine said under his breath. He removed a loose brick, then took out the key, opened the door, and let himself in.

A little white poodle ran to the front door barking in a high-pitched yap; then, recognizing her owner, the bark stopped, and her tail began wagging excitedly. She lay down and turned over on her back.

"Damn, Sherry, are you still spreading your legs for just any man who comes along?" Brandywine teased.

He knelt down to pet her. Sherry jumped up on him and began licking his face. Brandywine picked her up and rubbed her behind her ears. "Yeah, yeah, I missed you too," he said. "Shh. We can't wake up Glenda."

Brandywine took Sherry to the sliding glass door at the back of the house, opened it, and let her outside. He stood there for a moment looking out over the back yard. Sherry did her business before coming back into the house.

Brandywine had been up for most of the night and he was hungry. Going into the kitchen, he opened the refrigerator door, found some ground beef, and began frying himself a hamburger. He made a small one for Sherry.

"Don't worry, baby dog," he said. "I haven't forgotten how much you like your own little hamburger."

"That hamburger is stinking up the whole house."

Brandywine looked toward the door of the kitchen and saw Glenda standing there. She was wearing an old, worn, pink flannel robe and blue, floppy slippers. Brown, disheveled hair framed her face.

"Home is the warrior," Brandywine said, leaning over to kiss her.

Glenda turned away to avoid the kiss. "You let Sherry track mud in," she said.

"How do you do that?" Brandywine asked.

"How do I do what?"

"Say every word in the same monotone."

"You should have used the leash and not let her get in the mud," Glenda said, not responding to his comment.

"Yeah, well, I'm sort of out of practice. I've been in Vietnam for a year, or haven't you noticed?"

"How long are you going to be home?"

"Forever I hope," Brandywine said. The hamburgers done now, he set the skillet off the burner. "Do we have any buns?"

"Use bread. I thought you said in your letter that you were going to have to go back."

"That's what Colonel Cleaver has put in my orders," Brandywine said. "But while I'm here, I plan to go to the Department of Army and see if I can get them changed."

"You won't be able to."

"Maybe not, but I can sure try," Brandywine said. He got two pieces of bread and then opened the refrigerator to look for mayonnaise. "Any mayonnaise?"

"I don't keep it when you aren't here," she said.

Brandywine found mustard and began spreading it on his sandwich. "Did you miss me?"

"It was your choice to go back."

"What do you mean it was my choice? I had orders sending me back."

"You could have resigned from the Army."

"Glenda, I have seventeen years in. You think I should resign after seventeen years?"

"You could get a good job working in the shipyard."

"I don't want a job working in the shipyard. I'm an aviator, not a riveter or whatever the hell they would have me doing. Besides that, I sold my book. In three more years, I'll be able to retire and write full time."

"I think you should get a job."

"No Cokes?"

"I don't keep . . ."

". . . Cokes when I'm not around, yeah, I know." He poured himself a glass of milk, then sat at the table and ate his hamburger and drank his milk. "Ahh," he said. "Do you know how good real milk tastes? I've had nothing but that reconstituted shit for a year."

Glenda didn't answer.

Sherry stood up on her hind legs then moved up to Brandywine. He broke off a little of her hamburger and gave it to her.

"I'll bet nobody has fed you like this since I left, have they?" he said to the little dog.

"She has a feeding bowl," Glenda said.

"Yeah, but she needs a little TLC," Brandywine said, breaking off another piece to feed her. "So, did you get us flight and hotel reservations for our trip to New York?"

"I'm not going to New York with you."

"What? Why not? Wouldn't the school let you off?"

"I didn't ask to get off."

"Oh."

Glenda turned and started back toward the bedroom. "Go to New York if you want to, but you are just wasting your time."

"What do you mean I'm wasting my time? Glenda, I sold my book! Don't you know what that means?"

"It means you sold a book," she said. "But you can't make a living from selling one book."

"Isn't there some saying about a long journey starting with just one step?"

"You are wasting your time," she said again.

"All right, so you didn't make hotel and flight reservations for us. Did you make them for me?"

"Since you'll be going alone, I figured you'd rather do it yourself," Glenda called back over her shoulder.

Shaking his head in frustration, Brandywine finished his hamburger before walking into his library.

How many times over the last year had he thought of this moment? He loved his library. It wasn't a fine or classic library, but it was a full one, with at least two thousand books. Many were paperback books, novels with no particular value other than their value to him. But over the years he had managed to collect several very old books, some more than one hundred years old, and it gave him a great deal of pleasure to read a book that someone may have read in the last century. He turned on the lights and gasped.

"Glenda!!!" He called out in confusion, anger, and frustration.

His books were gone. Not one book remained. In their places on the bookshelves were potted plants, figurines, photographs, and bric-a-brac.

"Glenda, where are my books?"

Glenda didn't answer him.

Brandywine hurried back into the bedroom and hearing the shower coming from the bathroom, he walked in and jerked open the shower curtain.

"Get out of here!" Glenda shouted, quickly trying to cover her nude body.

"Oh, for Chrissake, Glenda, we are married," Brandywine said.

For all her dourness, she did have a beautiful shape, and Brandywine looked at it hungrily. For just a moment he remembered the early days back in Germany where they had neither radio nor TV, and they entertained themselves by innovative lovemaking at nights and on the weekends.

He smiled. "Come to think of it, we *are* married," he said. "How about I take a shower with you?" He stared unbuttoning his tunic.

Glenda jerked the curtain closed.

"Get out of here," she said.

"Glenda, for crying out loud . . . I've been gone for a year."

"We need to talk," Glenda said.

"Yes, we do. Oh!" Brandywine suddenly realized why he had come in here. "Where are my books? Why did you take them out of the library? Do you have them boxed up somewhere?"

"I burned them."

"What?" Brandywine asked. He jerked the curtain open. "Did you say you burned them?"

This time Glenda made no attempt to cover her nudity nor did she shut the curtain. She just stood there in the shower with the water cascading down from her small, but beautifully formed breasts. One drop hung from a nipple and glistened in the bathroom light.

"Yes."

Brandywine was thunderstruck. He wanted to yell and scream. But all he felt was an empty, sick, sinking sensation in the pit of his stomach.

"Why, Glenda?" he asked quietly. "Why did you burn my books?"

"They smelled musty," she said. She turned off the shower and reached for the towel.

Brandywine put the lid down on the toilet and sat. When he did, Sherry stood up on her back legs, and Brandywine leaned down to let her kiss him.

"W.W.," Glenda said as she wrapped the towel around herself. "I want a divorce."

Chapter Five

Brandywine waited as the other divorce cases before his were being dispatched. Outside, a cold, drizzling rain was falling, and he stared at the drops of rain as they made rivulet tracks down the dirty, gray windows. Very close to where he was sitting, a steam radiator hissed quietly, sending out an envelope of heat that left some areas of the courtroom too hot and other areas too cold.

Looking around, Brandywine saw Glenda on the opposite side of the room. She was sitting alone, still wearing her coat. She was clutching her purse on her lap, and though she wasn't actually in a fetal position, the way she was drawn up into herself gave Brandywine that impression. She stared straight ahead, her lips drawn into a tight line. Once he saw her lift a wadded tissue to dab at her eyes.

Glenda was crying and that surprised him. She rarely laughed and seldom cried. He suddenly experienced an overwhelming wave of sadness for a promise lost, and he felt a sense of pity for her. This couldn't be easy for her. For one quick, irrational moment, he thought about going over to her and asking her if she wanted to call this whole divorce thing off.

But he resisted the urge. This marriage had been going down hill for at least two years. In fact, he could remember being at the airport in Newport News, just before he left for Vietnam. He had watched a sergeant with his wife and daughter and saw them crying as they kissed him good-bye. Glenda did not come to the airport with him, and his dog's good-bye had been much more heartfelt than hers.

No, it would serve nothing to go to her now. Even if she agreed to call this off, it would only prolong the agony. He turned his attention back to the rain-streaked window.

"Bailiff, would you publish the next case, please," the judge said.

"Your Honor, there comes now a bill of divorcement from the plaintiff, Glenda Marie Brandywine, against her husband, Walter Winchell Brandywine, Mister Brandywine being a member of the United States Army," the bailiff said.

"Is plaintiff represented by counsel?"

A tall, thin man, with a prominent Adam's apple and a rather large nose, stood up. "She is, Your Honor. I am Carl Garrison, counsel for the plaintiff."

"Is the defendant represented by counsel?"

"No, sir, uh, Your Honor," Brandywine said.

"Mister Brandywine ..." the Judge started. "I see you are in uniform. What is the proper form of address?"

"Mister is correct, Your Honor. I am a warrant officer."

"Mister Brandywine, you do realize that you can have a lawyer?"

"Yes, Your Honor," Brandywine said.

"And you waive that right?"

"I do, Your Honor."

"Very well. Take the stand."

Brandywine was sworn in. He then sat in a chair beside the judge's bench. Garrison approached him.

"Mister Brandywine, have we spoken?"

"Yes."

Garrison took out a pair of horn-rimmed glasses and put them on, hooking them very carefully over one ear at a time. He opened a manila folder. "I am going to read this to you and see if now, in this court, you will testify that this agreement is right and correct in all details."

"It's right," Brandywine said. "Let's just get this over with."

The lawyer held up his hand. "Please, Mister Brandywine, allow me." The lawyer cleared his throat.

"I, Walter Winchell Brandywine, do grant, without contest, the divorce requested by Glenda Marie Brandywine. In the matter of property, I grant her full possession and ownership of a 1966 blue Ford Mustang. Do you so agree?"

"Yes."

"I grant full ownership and possession of a 1968 gold Oldsmobile Cutlass. Do you so agree?"

"Yes."

"I grant her full equity in the house located at 507 Lucas Creek Road, Newport News, Virginia, with the stipulation that from henceforth she will be responsible for the house payments. Do you so agree?"

"Yes."

"I grant her full possession and ownership of all furnishings therein. Do you so agree?"

"Yes."

"And finally, I grant her full ownership and possession of any and all stocks, bonds, and/or savings certificates as she may now own, or that you may own jointly or separately. Do you so agree?"

"Yes."

"Mister Brandywine," the judge asked, interrupting the lawyer. "Is your wife pregnant?"

"If she is, it is not by me," Brandywine said. There was a ripple of subdued laughter in the courtroom.

"Your Honor, we will stipulate that Glenda Marie Brandywine is not pregnant," the lawyer said. "Mister Brandywine has been in Vietnam for the last year."

"I see," the judge said. "Mister Brandywine, counsel for the plaintiff has read off a list of things that are going to your wife. What do you want from this marriage?"

"Me, Your Honor. I just want out."

Now the gallery laughed out loud.

The judge looked at Brandywine, nodded, and slammed his gavel down.

"Divorce granted," he said.

Brandywine noticed that the elevator operator was looking at him in the mirror, and because it made him a little uncomfortable, he held up his hat and made a pretense of examining the insignia of his rank, a single silver bar divided across the center by a brown bar.

"You look very handsome in your Army suit," the elevator operator said. There was just the hint of a lilt in his voice.

Brandywine cleared his throat but didn't answer.

"If you are going to be around later tonight, maybe we could have a drink together. You could tell me what it is like to sleep in a barracks with all those men and take showers together."

"I don't think so," Brandywine said, moving into the back corner.

When the elevator reached the lobby, Brandywine stepped out of it and walked away quickly. He saw several copies of the *New York Times*, neatly displayed in little clear plastic envelopes which read, "For Algonquin Hotel Guests Only - Welcome to New York."

Picking up a paper, he found a chair near one of the support pillars where he could keep an eye on the door. For the next several minutes he sat there, reading quietly.

"You have some nerve," a woman said, her voice dripping with vitriol.

Brandywine looked up from his paper.

"I beg your pardon, ma'am, am I sitting in the wrong place?" He stood. "I'll be happy to move."

"Anywhere you are is the wrong place," the woman said, spitefully. "How dare you come in here? Are you proud of all the babies you've killed?"

"Well no, ma'am, not all of them," Brandywine replied. "To tell the truth, most of 'em are just too damn little, and I have to throw them back. But every now and then I do manage to get one that's trophy size."

"You pig! You stinking rotten pig!" the woman said, shuddering in horror. "You are disgusting. Absolutely disgusting!"

"So what you are saying is even if I buy you drinks

and a nice meal, chances are you won't go to bed with me. Is that right?"

"What? You are a perfect . . . perfect horror of a man!" the woman said, her voice getting more and more shrill.

"Yes, ma'am," Brandywine said. "Well, perfection has always been my motto."

The woman turned and walked away, mumbling in barely controlled rage.

"You have a nice day now, ma'am. Ya' hear?" Brandywine called to her.

As the woman exited the lobby through the street door, a tall, thin, dapper-looking man came in. He was carrying an umbrella in one hand and a briefcase in the other. He held the door open for the woman, who made no effort to thank him. He looked into the lobby and seeing Brandywine, he smiled.

Damn, Brandywine thought. Is everybody in this town a fruit?

The man started toward him, and Brandywine wished the woman would come back.

"You must be Walter," the man said, extending his hand. "I don't know how many other Army officers are staying at the Algonquin today.

Brandywine returned the smile and extended his hand as well. This had to be Sam Silverman.

Nobody ever called him Walter. Even his family called him W.W., and he preferred that his friends call him Brandywine. But if his editor wanted to call him

Walter, he wasn't going to correct him. He could call him anything he wanted.

"Mister Silverman," Brandywine said.

"Please, it's Sam. So, you made it home from Vietnam, I see. All safe and sound."

"For the moment," Brandywine said.

"I beg your pardon?"

"I couldn't get an early drop, so I had to agree to return to Vietnam for six more months."

Sam looked shocked. "You have to go back? I thought you said that it wouldn't be difficult coming home early."

"Yeah," Brandywine said. "That's what I thought too. But my colonel had other ideas. I have a thirty day chargeable leave, then I must return," he added.

"That's awful," Sam said. He looked at his watch. "Well, we're to meet Ralph Day at the Lambs Club for lunch. I think we'd better go."

It wasn't raining hard, though it was sprinkling when they got outside, and Sam opened his umbrella and tried to hold it over both of them. Brandywine moved to get out from under it. Sam moved to put him under it, and Brandywine moved again until he was actually walking in the street alongside the curb.

It wasn't until then that Sam, who had been engaged in conversation, realized that Brandywine had been trying to pull away from him.

"What are your doing?" Sam asked. "Why are you walking in the street like that?"

"Oh, uh, force of habit, I guess," Brandywine said. "Too many chances for ambush from the buildings."

Brandywine didn't have the nerve to tell him the real reason was that he just did not want to walk under an umbrella.

"Wow!" Sam said, impressed by the answer. "Yes, I guess you guys who face death every day do get used to such things, don't you? But, I assure you, you don't have to worry about an ambush in downtown Manhattan." He chuckled then added, "Wait a minute, what am I talking about? Of course you do. You just don't have to worry about being ambushed by the VC. Oh, there's a taxi."

In the taxi, Sam told Brandywine a little about Ralph Day.

"He is the publisher at Foster Crescent," Sam said. "Foster is a very old and much respected house. They published Fitzgerald, Hemingway, and James Jones among others. And Ralph Day is the first non-family member to head up the house."

When they reached the Lambs Club, Brandywine went inside the restaurant while Sam hung back to pay the driver. There were two men standing just inside the door and when Sam came in, he greeted both of them.

"Hello, Ralph," Sam said. "I see you got here just a little ahead of us. This is our author, Walter Brandywine."

"Walter," Ralph said. "It's good to meet you. He

turned to the man he had been talking to. "This is Joseph Heller."

Brandywine gasped. "*Catch-22*?" He stuck his hand out. "What a great book!"

"Thank you," Heller replied. "So, you are in the Army I see. And you are an author?"

"Yes, well, soon to be an author," Brandywine said. "I just sold a book to Pendarrow House."

"What's your book about?"

"It's much like yours, Joe," Sam said. "A rather iconoclastic look at the military."

"Well, then I shall certainly look forward to reading it," Heller said. "Ralph, I'll call you later."

"Yes, take care," Ralph said, holding up his hand. Then turning to Sam and Brandywine, he said, "Shall we? Our table is just over there."

Brandywine followed Sam and Ralph into the dining room. He saw James Whitmore sitting at one of the other tables engaged in conversation with his dinner partner. Brandywine wanted to speak to him, but he didn't know the ethics of approaching famous people in restaurants, so he did nothing.

"Good move," Sam said.

"What?"

"Not going over to bother Mister Whitmore."

Brandywine laughed. "Was I that obvious?"

"You were that non-New Yorker," Sam replied with a chuckle.

"Sergeant Kinnie."

"What?"

"He played Sergeant Kinnie in the movie, *Battleground*. That was back in 1950. That's been twenty years and he hasn't changed. I don't know if he looked old then or young now."

"He was born looking like that," Ralph said. "All actors are."

When both Sam and Ralph ordered the special, which was baked salmon, Brandywine ordered the same thing, though he would have preferred something else. For the first few minutes after they ordered, and even after the meal arrived, Sam and Ralph spoke knowingly about the business. Brandywine sat quietly, and while he didn't particularly enjoy his food, he did appreciate this unique opportunity to eavesdrop on "inside" talk about books and writers. He listened carefully for the little tidbits of information that he would be able to drop into future conversations.

Then he heard a shocker.

"He took his boyfriend with him," Ralph said, talking about a writer whose name Brandywine recognized. "I told him, 'Look, if you are going to be signing books in New York, Boston, or San Francisco, it is perfectly okay to have your boyfriend sit at the table with you. But for heaven's sake, don't do it in Jackson, Mississippi.'"

Sam laughed and Brandywine, getting over his shock that the author they were talking about, a well-known writer of gritty private eye books could be gay, laughed with him.

Ralph looked across the table at Brandywine. "Please forgive us for carrying on a private conversation, but we don't get a chance to visit that much, and as I'm sure you've just noticed, editors do love to gossip."

"That's all right; I've enjoyed listening in, sort of like a fly on the wall."

"Well, to begin with, welcome home. Glad to see you got through it safely."

"The damnedest thing," Sam said. "He has to go back to Vietnam."

"What? You have to go back? When, and why?"

"I have just over a week left on this leave, and then I have to go back for six months," Brandywine said. "It was the only way I could come to New York to take care of this."

"What is that going to do for your publicity campaign?" Ralph asked Sam.

"It's going to force some changes, but it might even work out better. War hero writes book about Vietnam, while serving in Vietnam. We'll even send someone over there to get a picture of him on duty so to speak, for the back of the book."

"I uh, wouldn't call myself a war hero," Brandywine said.

"Nonsense," Sam said. He pointed to the four

rows of ribbons above Brandywine's left breast pocket. "What are these ribbons?"

"Bronze Star, Air Medal, Purple Heart, Meritorious Service Medal, Army Commendation Medal," Brandywine said. "The rest are 'been there,' ribbons."

"Sounds pretty heroic to me," Sam said. He looked across the table at Ralph. "So, what do you think, Ralph? Do you think Foster Crescent is up to doing the paperback release of this hero's book?"

"Walter, tell me what the book is about," Ralph said.

"Oh, uh, I thought you had already read the manuscript."

"I have, but let's assume that I haven't," Ralph said. "Let's assume I'm a television interviewer, and you are on my TV show. Tell me, Mister Brandywine, what is your book about?"

"Well, it's about this five hundred dollar rat and . . . uh . . . no, wait, it's about this helicopter pilot who. . . no, wait, it's about . . .," Brandywine started and stopped several times, obviously floundering about as he tried to explain the book.

"Wait a minute," Ralph said. Putting his fork down, he picked up a matchbook from the ashtray in the middle of the table. He tore the matches out and handed the cover to Brandywine.

"I'll tell you what. If you can write what your book

is about on the back of this matchbook cover, I'll buy it," he said.

"You're kidding, right? You want me to condense my entire book down to just what I can put on the back of this matchbook cover?"

"Oh, yes, I'm very serious."

Brandywine looked over at Sam, and Sam handed him his pen.

Brandywine examined the pen. It was beautiful, the main body a cobalt blue, the clasp, head, and point made of what he was sure, was real gold. He compared this pen to the simple, black, ballpoint pens he used in the Army.

He wrote:

Brandywine's War is a picaresque novel of the war in Vietnam. It chronicles one man's efforts to survive an insane war, by always staying one step ahead of the insanity. It combines ribald humor with gut-wrenching pathos.

He handed the pen to Sam and the matchbook cover to Ralph.

Ralph read the matchbook cover without comment or facial expression; he handed it to Sam.

Sam read it, and nodded. "Very good," Sam said.

"Thirty?" Ralph asked.

"It's a deal," Sam agreed. He looked at Brandywine. "Walter, congratulations. You now have a hard and soft-cover deal."

"Damn!" Brandywine said with a broad smile. "Not too many days ago I was crawling around in a muddy rice paddy just outside Tay Ninh recovering a downed helicopter. Now I'm sitting in a plush club in the middle of New York, hobnobbing with a famous author and a famous movie actor and talking a book deal with two big-time New York editors. Damn, this is almost perfect."

"Only almost?" Ralph asked, chuckling.

"Yeah," Brandywine said. He looked at the mostly uneaten salmon on his plate. "It would've been perfect if I had ordered a hamburger and a Coke. Anything but this shit. God, I hate fish."

Sam and Ralph laughed out loud. Sam then held up his hand and called a waiter over.

"Yes, sir?"

"Take this 'shit' out of here, and bring this gentleman a hamburger," Sam said.

"And a Coke," Ralph added.

Chapter Six

Brandywine thought it was somewhat fitting that the Warrant Officer Aviation Career Branch was not in the Pentagon with all other career branches but was located in a temporary building at Fort McNair, Virginia, across the Potomac from the Pentagon. You could see the Pentagon from here . . . but this wasn't the Pentagon. He looked through magazines as he waited to talk to his career counselor.

A sergeant came into the room.

"Mister Brandywine?"

"Yes," Brandywine said, setting the magazine aside.

"Mister Tadlock will see you now, sir."

"Thank you."

Brandywine went into the little office where he

was greeted by a warrant who reminded him of Yul Brynner.

"Mister Brandywine," he said. "Welcome to Warrant Officer Aviation Branch. Have you ever been here before?"

Brandywine shook his head. "No, I've spoken to some of the people here on the telephone, but this is the first time I've ever actually been here."

"I'd never been here either until I got this assignment," Tadlock said.

"How do you like it?"

"It's expensive, but it does have its perks." Suddenly, Tadlock chuckled. "So, tell me, Mister Brandywine, do you still play *Tijuana Taxi* on your trumpet?"

"I'll be damned," he said. "Don't tell me you were one of my students in the Aviation Maintenance Officers' Course."

"Yep. I went through AMOC three years ago," Tadlock said. "You used the trumpet to . . . somehow explain propeller governors . . . though I never quite got the connection."

Brandywine laughed. "It was to demonstrate valves and how they work to redirect the flow of air or fluids," he said, moving his fingers in the way of a trumpet player. "But the truth is the connection was strained at best. I just wanted to show you folks that I'm not only a pretty face; I can also play the trumpet."

"Well, if what I heard was any indication of your musical talent . . . don't give up your warrant," Tadlock said, good naturedly. "Have a seat."

As Brandywine took the proffered chair, Tadlock picked up a rather thick file folder.

"You did eighteen months on your first tour?"

"Yes."

"Why? Twelve months is normal."

"I got an involuntary six month extension because of a shortage of qualified maintenance officers in the Thirty-fourth Group," Brandywine said. "But because of that, they allowed me to choose my stateside assignment.

"And you've been in country for eleven months of this tour."

"Eleven months and fourteen days," Brandywine said.

"And as I understand it, you volunteered to extend for six more months just to get a thirty day leave when you had only sixteen days remaining to complete your tour?"

"Yes."

"Why in the hell would you do something like that?"

"I sold a book. The publisher wanted me to come home to meet the editor and sign the contract for residual rights, and time was of the essence. I tried to get an early drop but couldn't get it approved."

"Why not?" Tadlock asked. "Thirty day early drops are routine now. Many are getting forty-five and some as much as sixty day early drops."

"You tell me why," Brandywine said. "But the only way I could come home early was to take a leave, and in order to do that I had to volunteer to extend for six more months."

"And you are here now, trying to get out of that additional six months. Is that right?" Tadlock asked.

There was the suggestion, though just the suggestion, of a tone of condemnation in Tadlock's voice.

"That's right," Brandywine said.

"Don't you think that is a violation of your agreement with the Army?"

"Mister Tadlock, the way I see it, the Army violated its agreement with me. The regulations say that anyone who volunteers for a six-month extension can have a non-charged thirty-day leave with transportation supplied. Colonel Cleaver specifically ordered that my leave be charged against my accrued time. Not only that . . . he also insisted that I pay my own transportation costs."

"I see, but you didn't pay your way back to the States, did you?"

"No, I did not. I managed to get orders cut appointing me as an armed courier. I had a briefcase handcuffed to my wrist for two days," he said. "It was most uncomfortable, but it did get me back to the States free. I have no idea what was in it."

"Would you like to know?"

Brandywine looked surprised. "You know what I carried?"

"Yes," Tadlock said. He looked at a paper in the file. "You carried a plea from the Saigon Sub-Post Commander for an increase in the allocation of condoms, a letter from the Chief of Chaplains, MACV, for ten thousand rosaries, and a request from the Vietnamese Minister of Culture to the Undersecretary of State for twenty-four tickets to *Oh Calcutta.*"

"Well," Brandywine said. "As long as I did my duty. So, what about getting my orders changed?"

Tadlock leaned back in his chair. "I'll tell you the truth, Brandywine, I had orders cut reassigning you to Fort Eustis, Virginia."

Brandywine smiled broadly, and stuck his hand out. "That's great! Thanks!"

Instead of shaking Brandywine's hand, Tadlock held his hand up, as if shielding himself.

"Not so fast," he said. "DA rescinded the orders."

"What? Why?"

"It seems your friend Colonel Cleaver anticipated that you might do something like this. So he wrote a letter to WOAVN Assignments Personnel insisting that you be returned in accordance with your agreement. Whatever you've got left to do in the States, I suggest you get it done. In five days you have to report back to the 65th Trans in Vietnam."

"No way of getting around it?"

"I'm afraid not."

Brandywine drummed his fingers on Tadlock's

desktop for a few seconds and sighed. "All right . . . I guess I'm stuck. Listen . . . I checked. A ticket from here to Saigon is going to cost me six hundred and sixty-six dollars. That's a lot of money. Do you think you could at least cut me travel orders?"

"I'd like to, but Colonel Cleaver took care of that, too," he said, sliding the letter across. "He really doesn't like you, does he? Read the bottom paragraph."

Orders should be cut specifically to indicate that subject WO is to travel at his own expense and should state that space available travel is not authorized.

"Damn," Brandywine said.

"Well, you are a rich author aren't you? I mean, you said you just sold a book."

"I don't have any of the money yet. And believe me . . . it's not going to make me rich."

"Wish I could help you."

"Maybe you can help me," he said.

"How?"

"When you cut the orders, make the travel part of it an addendum . . . and put that addendum on a second page."

Tadlock squinted his eyes in question. "What good will that do? You'll have to show your travel orders at Oakland."

"Yes, but not in Honolulu. There, all I need for space available are my routing orders. I'll just lose page two."

Tadlock laughed. "Son of a bitch," he said. "You know what, that might work after all. Okay, I'll do it. Anything else I can do?"

"Can you cut retroactive TDY orders for the last thirty days? That way, at least, the time here won't count against my leave time."

Tadlock nodded. "I'll not only do that. I'll give you per diem at fifteen dollars a day. That won't completely offset your travel expenses, but it will help."

"WOPA!" Brandywine said, holding his hand up for a high-five.

"WOPA!" Tadlock replied.

WOPA was Warrant Officer Protective Association, and it meant that, whenever possible, one warrant would always help another.

"Hey, Brandywine," Tadlock said.

"Yes?"

"There is one thing you can do for me."

"What?"

"When the book comes out, I want an autographed copy."

"You've got it, brother," Brandywine said.

He left Fort McNair in an ebullient mood, and it wasn't until he got into the car that he realized the truth.

He was going back to Vietnam.

Chapter Seven

Tan San Nhut had not changed. The hot, sticky air was permeated by the stench of the burning honey pots. An F4 took off, and when hitting its afterburner, rocketed into the sky on twin pillars of flame.

The Army shared Tan San Nhut with the Air Force, and even some Navy units. A Dust-Off helicopter passed just overhead, shooting a landing for Hotel-3, where an Army ambulance stood by, waiting to rush the wounded to the hospital.

Hooch girls were jabbering with each other as they took care of outside tasks.

Sweat stained the back of Brandywine's shirt and pooled under his armpits. He had been wearing this same short-sleeve khaki uniform for three days now, and it had gone beyond rank long ago.

Brandywine dropped his duffle bag next to the large fifty-five gallon drum filled with sand, which bore the printed sign:

CLEAR WEAPONS BEFORE ENTERING BUILDING

The orderly room hooch was like all the other buildings in the company area: wood half way up, then screen wire for the top half. Shutters were held open by supports so they could be dropped during the monsoons. Brandywine knew from experience that the shutters did not keep out the rain but did keep out the air so that most of the time nobody ever bothered to drop them, even in the most torrential downpour.

Brandywine pushed the screen door open and stepped inside. He heard the intermittent clack of a typewriter, frequently interrupted so that a mumbling clerk could make a generous application of a white, correcting paste.

The first sergeant looked up.

"Can I help you, Chief?" he asked.

"Where's Sergeant Coty?"

"If you mean where is Private Coty, his ass is in the Long Binh Jail. I'm First Sergeant now. I'm First Sergeant Muldoon. What can I do for you?"

"I'm W.W. Brandywine, and I'm . . ."

"Son of a bitch!" Muldoon said happily as he

stood and stuck out his hand. "Am I glad to see you! Mister Brandywine, you just won me two-hundred dollars."

"Let me guess. You bet that I would come back."

"Yeah, I . . . " Muldoon started to say but then he chuckled. "How'd you know?"

"I figured there would be a pool running," he said. "Only I figured Coty would be running it."

"He is the one who started it," Muldoon said.

"I'm glad you won two-hundred dollars, but I have to tell you, I tried like hell not to come back."

"Yes, sir, we all knew you would. And, even though I'm glad I won the money, I have to confess that I'm a little disappointed to see you here. You're a legend around here . . . the way you manage to manipulate things. A secret part of me was hoping you could pull this one off."

"Remember, Top, not even Ted Williams batted a thousand," Brandywine said.

"You got that right."

"Is Major Casey in?"

"He's in there . . . working on his tinfoil. Won't do you any good to go see him, though."

"Oh? Why's that?"

First Sergeant Muldoon pulled open a file cabinet and took out a folder. "You've been reassigned. You aren't in the 65th anymore."

"I'm not? Where am I?"

"So far there haven't been any new orders cut for

you. You are supposed to report directly to Colonel Cleaver for further assignment."

"Oh shit."

"He wants you to report to him as soon as you get back."

"All right," Brandywine said. "But I'm going to stick my head in and say hello to Major Casey first. Then I'm going to walk down to the supply room. How's Sergeant Gibson? He is still here, isn't he?"

"I guess it depends on what you mean by still here. He hasn't drawn a sober breath since I arrived three weeks ago."

"Who is running Supply?"

"Miss Song and the new Property Book Officer."

"Oh? Who replaced me as PBO?"

"Unsoldier."

"What? Unsoldier is now the PBO? Wait a minute. How can Unsoldier be a Property Book Officer?"

"Beats me, but from all I can determine, he's doing a pretty good job of it. I mean, no offense to you, Mister Brandywine."

Brandywine laughed. "No offense taken," he said. Brandywine stepped over to the door marked Commanding Officer and knocked lightly.

"Come in," a muffled voice called.

When he stepped inside, Brandywine saw an enormous ball of tinfoil sitting on the desk. The ball was at least five feet in diameter, so big that Major Casey, who was sitting behind it, couldn't even be seen. That is he couldn't be seen to be identified. But Brandywine could see his hands as they reached around the side to carefully apply another strip of foil.

"Did you bring me any foil?" a disembodied voice asked from behind the big, silver ball.

"Of course I did. Did you think I would come see you without bringing you any tinfoil?"

"Brandywine?"

There was the sound of a chair being moved. A moment later, Major Casey's head appeared around the edge of the silver ball.

"Damn, it is you. Oh, hell, I just lost fifty bucks."

"Sorry," Brandywine said. "I tried to win it for you." He pulled out a large handful of chewing gum wrappers with the foil still attached.

"You aren't here anymore," Casey said as he took the foil. "Did Muldoon tell you?"

"He told me."

"I hate to lose you."

"Who has been flying the recovery missions?"

"B. Dowling Mudd and some FNG."

Brandywine smiled, broadly. "Well, I'm glad. You can't get a better man than B. Dowling Mudd. Who's the new guy?"

Casey started tearing off the tiny tinfoil strips and put them onto the large ball of foil.

"His name is Kirby."

"Kirby? I don't recognize the name."

"You wouldn't. He got here the day you left."

"Is he a warrant officer?"

"No, he's a first lieutenant, and a first class horse's ass," Casey said, now so intently into the task at hand that Brandywine had already receded into the background.

When Brandywine stepped out of Casey's office, he almost ran into Captain Fender.

"You are to report to Colonel Cleaver," Fender said. He punctuated his comment with a sniff on his inhaler.

"So I've been told."

"All of your shenanigans are coming back on you now. Sniff, snert."

"What shenanigans?" Brandywine asked.

"You know what shenanigans. Snert, snit, sniff. Did you go to Washington to try and get out of your responsibility to come back to Vietnam? Snit, sniff, snit, snark."

Captain Fender used an inhaler so continuously that Brandywine insisted to anyone who would listen that he stored it in his left nostril. When he held it in his hand, he wasn't sticking it in his nostril. He was merely removing it to use somewhere else, and after he used it somewhere else, he would return it to its normal place, his left nostril.

"As a matter of fact, I did," Brandywine said.

Fender smiled. "It didn't work, I see. The fabled Brandywine machinations failed you. Sniff!" he added, in a hard punctuation.

"No . . . the fabled Brandywine machinations didn't work," Brandywine admitted. "If you'll excuse me now, Captain, I have to report to my new duty station."

"You go ahead," Fender said. "I think you'll find that Colonel Cleaver won't put up with you the way Major Casey did."

Brandywine started to leave, but just before he reached the door, he turned and called back to Captain Fender, who was going into his office.

"Oh, by the way, while I was at the Pentagon, I ran into Colonel Hedrick. Has he contacted you yet?"

"Colonel Hedrick? Sniff? Contacted me about what?"

Brandywine held out his hand and shook his head. "Oh, it's not my place to tell you," he said. "But I'll say this. If you get the assignment he's talking about, you are one lucky dog."

"What assignment? Snert?"

"I can't tell you. But when you get there, hobnobbing with all those high-powered people, I just hope you remember who your friends are."

"What are you talking about? We aren't friends."

"That's all I can tell you for now," Brandywine said.

As Brandywine stepped out of the orderly room, Fender was still standing at the door to his own office, a look of confused concern on his face.

"Sniff?"

Brandywine wanted to say hello to Gibson and Miss Song before he reported to Colonel Cleaver to find out what his new duty would be, so when he left the orderly room, he walked through the company area toward the supply room. He passed by a twittering group of mamasans who were wearing handkerchiefs around their nose to blot out the smell as they burned the contents of the honeypots they had pulled out from the latrines.

Sergeant Percival, the NCOIC of the shit burners and rat catchers, saw Brandywine and he came to attention.

"Attention, Ladies!" Percival said, saluting Brandywine with a hand that quivered just over his right eyebrow. The women continued their chatter and shit burning, paying no attention to him. "Good morning, Mister Brandywine. It's good to have you back in country!"

"Hello, Sergeant Percival," Brandywine said, returning the salute.

"I got it, Mister Brandywine!" Percival said proudly. "I got my medal for killing rats . . . just like you said I would."

Sergeant Percival was Vector Control NCO. Ever the conscientious soldier, Percival submitted carefully worded reports on the amount of defecation burned and on the total number of rats captured and killed each day.

Percival submitted his reports to USARV RAT CONTROL COMMAND. There was no such headquarters. In a practical joke that had turned more cruel than he ever intended, Brandywine had created the office as well as the demand that daily reports be submitted.

But the joke nearly backfired when Brandywine put a tag reading RT-209 on one of the dead rats. He followed that by generating a letter promising to pay five hundred dollars for the return of "Marsha," a test rodent bearing the identification tag, RT-209.

When Percival ran to the office proudly holding up the tag screaming in joy over his windfall, Brandywine produced a letter from USARV RAT CONTROL COMMAND saying that the funds would not be disbursed for a deceased rodent.

In frustrated rage, Percival grabbed a .45 pistol and started after the Vietnamese Papasan responsible for killing the rat. Brandywine chased Percival down, tackling him just in time to prevent his joke from going tragically wrong.

A few days later Brandywine saw that Percival had recovered from his disappointment. Percival was working diligently with his rat traps, talking and arguing with Papasan who squatted alongside him. Apparently the two men had resolved their differences and were now working happily together. A pillar of black oily smoke that was rising from the burning honey-buckets told Brandywine that Percival's other main duty had been efficiently seen to as well.

Watching the two of them, Brandywine had felt both ashamed and proud. For a moment the strangeness of pride was an emotion he couldn't explain even to himself. Yet of all the crazy people in this war, out of all the idiocy, Sergeant Percival was the only man Brandywine could point to as a man of definite accomplishment.

Sergeant Percival was killing rats, quickly and thoroughly. His efforts in Vietnam accomplished two things that the total American commitment had not done. Percival was benefiting mankind by eliminating a disease carrier, and his progress could easily be marked in the very real and tangible fact that rats in the 65th were no longer a problem.

Brandywine resolved that day to get Percival the Army Commendation Medal. He was glad to see that the recommendation had gone through.

"Good for you, Sergeant Percival."

"You got it for me, Sir."

Brandywine shook his head. "No, Sergeant. I didn't get it for you. You earned it."

Brandywine continued his walk. The supply room was at the opposite end of the company area from the orderly room, and as Brandywine approached it, he saw a few soldiers standing around the side at the open DX window. The Direct Exchange window was open one hour per day to allow soldiers to turn in old, worn equipment and clothing for new equipment and clothing.

Brandywine had been proud of what he had been able to do with the supply office. When he took it over, it was little more than a Quonset hut shell over a cement pad, and he turned it into a comfortable, and if he did say so himself, rather handsome office. And while he was not at all happy to be back in country, he was looking forward to seeing the office again.

But when he stepped inside he was amazed by the changes that had occurred in just thirty days. Hundreds of strings of colored beads hung from the ceiling, a marble fountain sat bubbling in the middle of the floor, black-lighted psychedelic posters decorated the walls, beanbag chairs had replaced the "Chairs, metal w/padded seats," and very low tables had replaced the "Desks, metal, six-Drawer."

The place reeked of incense, and from a speaker came the sound of sitar music. In addition to Miss Song, there were four new Vietnamese women. All the women, including Miss Song, wore very, very short mini-skirts and halter-tops. Their midriffs were bare.

"Mister Blandeewine, you back in country!" Miss Song squealed happily. She ran to him and threw her arms around him. "I think maybe you no come back."

"I tried not to," Brandywine said, looking around

the supply room. He held out his hand, taking it all in. "Uh, when did all this happen?"

"It happen when Unsolder become new PBO," Miss Song said.

"Yes, I heard that. You mean he really is the PBO?"

"Yes sir."

Where is he?"

"Unsoldier back there," Miss Song said, pointing to an area that was draped off by long, hanging sheets of yellow and red silk. "But you no can see until eleven hundred. He do his meditation now."

"His meditation? Okay, what about Sergeant Gibson? Where is he?"

Miss Song pointed but said nothing. It wasn't until then that Brandywine saw that there was a bare foot and naked leg sticking up from behind one of the beanbag chairs. When he walked over to investigate, he found Gibson in his underwear, passed out behind the large puff of Naugahyde. He was holding a whiskey bottle, which had a baby-bottle nipple at the top.

"Sergeant Gibson?"

At the sound of his name, Gibson stirred.

"ETS?" Gibson asked.

"No, you have a little more than two years until you reach your End Tour of Service."

"Tell me when it is my ETS," Gibson said. He brought the bottle up to his lips and began nursing.

"Damn," Brandywine said. "He's always been a drunk, but how long has he been like this?"

"Since Unsoldier take over," Miss Song said. When she saw the worried look on Brandywine's face, she reached out to touch him on the shoulder. "But you not worry, Mister Blandeewine," she said. "I takey good care of Sargee Gibson for you. He make his retirement."

"Thanks," Brandywine said. "Oh, and thanks for signing me out when I took my leave."

"Is okay. I can sign your name numbah one."

"Yeah . . . remind me never to let you get hold of my check book."

"Meeting for book go good?"

"Yes, very good."

"Meeting with wife-American go good? Beau coups makee love, I bet. Long time no see, beau coups horney."

Brandywine shook his head, slowly.

"Not good?" Miss Song said, the tone of her voice showing her concern.

"It depends on what you call good, and not good," Brandywine said. "We are divorced."

"If wife-American not love you, then is good you divorce. Now you can marry again. Maybe wife— Vietnamee or another wife-American."

"Yeah, well, I'm not exactly looking for another wife just yet," Brandywine said.

Brandywine started toward the area Miss Song had identified as Unsoldier's inner sanctum.

"Oh, Mister Blandeewine, Unsoldier not likee you go back there," Miss Song said in alarm.

Brandywine waved her off as he jerked the sheets aside. "Unsoldier, are you in here?" he asked.

Unsoldier was sitting in the lotus position, his arms out, palms up, and eyes closed. He was wearing a Purple Nehru jacket. There were several gold chains hanging around his neck, his hair and beard were neatly trimmed, and his fingernails perfectly manicured. This was in stark contrast to the first time Brandywine had seen Unsoldier. Then, he was a thin scarecrow with a ragged beard and long unkempt hair.

Unsolder was humming softly to himself.

"Hmmmmmm, hmmmmmm, hmmmmmm, hmmmmm."

"Unsoldier?" Brandywine said.

Unsoldier stopped his humming, and opened his eyes.

"Ah, Mister Brandywine, you are back, I see," he said. "And how was your sojourn into the bowels of the great Gotham? I trust your book contract was successfully negotiated."

Not only had Unsoldier's appearance changed, so had his diction. He had given up his Hippie patois for the more sophisticated idiom of a college graduate. And, if the degree posted on the wall behind

Unsoldier was real, Unsoldier had an MBA from the University of California at Berkley.

"Yes, it went well. What is all this?" Brandywine asked, taking in everything with a wave of his hand. "What have you done to my supply room?"

"Oh, haven't you heard? It isn't your supply room anymore," Unsoldier said. "You will be getting a new assignment from Colonel Cleaver."

Brandywine let out a sigh as he ran his hand through his hair. "What the hell . . . does everyone know I'm getting a new assignment from Cleaver?"

"Call him Ishmael. You are his white whale," Unsoldier said.

"It's been a long time since I read the book. Tell me, Unsoldier, who won? Captain Ahab or Moby Dick?"

Unsoldier held up his finger and tried to look inscrutable. "Oh, I think we will just have to let this little drama play out."

"You're right . . . it isn't my supply room anymore," he said. "But, what have you done to it?"

"It is called ergonomics," Unsoldier said. "I have simply created a much more user-friendly work atmosphere. Don't you like it?"

"It's all right, I suppose. But I'm confused."

"What confuses you, my son?"

"You aren't an officer. You aren't an NCO. You aren't anything. You are an unsoldier. So, how did you become the Property Book Officer?"

"Somebody had to do it," Unsoldier replied, as if that answered the question.

Brandywine left the supply room and walked down to the flight line. So far today, he felt like Alice in Wonderland. He needed a little stability, and Chief Warrant Officer B. Dowling Mudd was the most stable individual he knew.

When Brandywine got to the hangar, he saw Specialist-6 Trapp working on the recovery helicopter, and he breathed a sigh of relief. At least, that hadn't changed.

Or had it?

The helicopter was now sporting a name, emblazoned on the pilot's door: KIRBY'S CHARIOT.

Underneath the name of the helicopter was a series of small helicopter silhouettes, painted in yellow. Brandywine wondered about it but decided he would just wait and ask B. Dowling Mudd.

Although the recovery office had not changed as much as the supply room had, Brandywine did notice several differences. The first and most obvious difference was a wall of eight by ten photographs that surrounded the large map of Vietnam. A string of red wool yarn stretched from each photograph to a spot on the map.

Stepping closer to the eight by ten glossies, Brandywine saw that each one of them was the picture of a lieutenant . . . always the same lieutenant, either standing by or holding a piece of a wrecked helicopter.

"Are you from PIO?" a voice asked. "Are you here to do a story about me?"

Turning away from the map, Brandywine saw a young lieutenant. This was the man who was in every picture.

"Uh, no," Brandywine said. "I'm W.W. Brandywine. Is B. Dowling Mudd around?"

"He's in Vung Tau for a couple of days."

"Oh, I'm sorry I missed him."

"W.W. Brandywine? Yes, I know who you are. You were the recovery officer, weren't you?"

"Yes."

"Well, I've got your old job now."

"Yes, I heard you were flying with B. Dowling Mudd."

"Get real," the young lieutenant said. "B. Dowling Mudd is just a warrant officer. I'm a commissioned officer. I'm not flying with him; B. Dowling Mudd is flying with me."

"You must be Kirby."

The lieutenant stuck his hand out. "Jefferson Fremont Kirby is my name, and killing VC is my game."

"Killing VC? I thought you were the recovery officer."

"For now," Kirby said. "For now."

Chapter Eight

The Red Bull Inn was a combination BOQ and Officers' Open Mess. Brandywine checked in with billeting and learned that his old room was still available, so he got it back. Then he took a shower and changed uniforms. He borrowed a jeep from the supply room so he could report to Colonel Cleaver, the Commanding Officer of the 365th Aviation Battalion. Headquarters for the 365th was on Tru Minh Ky Street, just across Railroad Track Number Eight, in an old mansion that belonged to a French rubber planter.

The house sat behind a high, stone fence topped with shards of broken bottles, nails, and razor wire. The front gate was guarded by White Mice and one of the white-uniformed Vietnamese policeman stepped out of the guardhouse as Brandywine approached the gate.

"You habbee trip tickee?" the policeman asked.

Brandywine showed him the trip ticket, and the policeman stepped back and saluted Brandywine as he drove onto the compound. The lawn was beautifully landscaped with sculptured shrubbery and alive with an aromatic and colorful profusion of flowers. It was being tended by two Vietnamese gardeners of indeterminate age. Neither of them looked up as Brandywine parked in the circular drive.

The house itself was a large, tan stucco edifice, two stories high, with a red tile roof. On the right side of the house was a porte-cochere where sat an olive drab Ford LTD staff car.

Brandywine exited the jeep and climbed the steps to the front porch. The front porch was well shaded and furnished with wicker chairs, tables and settees.

Right here, inside this compound, on the porch of this beautiful old plantation, it was very hard to realize that on the other side of the high walls was a city whose population had increased almost tenfold in the last twenty years. The newly arrived people moved into one-room hovels with relatives, or added onto existing structures, little shanties of flattened beer cans that pushed out into the already crowded lanes and alleyways. Streets that were once broad enough to allow a double stream of cars had been turned into narrow, twisting labyrinths, barely wide enough to allow a walking man passage. Among these structures, and behind them, in dark, damp corners in the intricate maze of paths, were the cubicles used for prostitution and dope dealing.

The alleys were dark even at high noon, because the overhang blotted out the sun. There were holes and passages leading from one alley to another, and through them, people would scurry about like moles through tunnels, sometimes going for weeks at a time without ever seeing the light of day.

On the other side of the wall were perpetrators and victims, filth and squalor. On this side of the wall was beauty and tranquility, reminiscent of the pre-war Saigon that was known as the "Paris of the Orient."

The scene changed again inside the house, for here was clearly a military headquarters, with telephones jangling, typewriters clacking, and busy soldiers wearing, not the jungle fatigues of the field soldier, but short-sleeved khaki uniforms complete with ribbons and a USARV patch which hung from the button of their left breast pocket. Such soldiers were called REMFs by the field soldiers.

Brandywine signed the visitor's log, noting his arrival at 0900. He walked over to the nearest clerk's desk where a specialist-5 was on duty.

"Yes sir, Chief, what can I do for you?" he asked.

"Specialist Clark is it?" Brandywine asked, reading the young clerk's nametag. "My name is W.W. Brandywine, and I'm here to see Colonel Cleaver."

"Sir, do you have an appointment?" Clark asked.

"An appointment? No."

Clark looked at the book for a moment; then he shook his head. "I'm sorry, Chief, but, if you don't have an appointment, Colonel Cleaver won't be able to see you."

"Okay," Brandywine said. He turned to walk away.

"Do you want me to make you an appointment?" Clark called after him.

"No," Brandywine said. "If the colonel wants to see me, I'm sure he will make an appointment."

Specialist Clark laughed. "I doubt that's going to happen, Mister Brandywine," he said. "I mean, I can't see a colonel making an appointment to see a warrant officer."

"I guess you're right," Brandywine said. "Foolish me."

He laughed as he drove out of the compound.

The Red Bull was fairly busy that night, packed with aviators, doctors, and nurses. Brandywine saw several familiar faces, including those he had never met, though he could remember having seen them in here before. But he also saw several new faces. That wasn't unusual since Vietnam was a constantly rotating cauldron of military personnel, some just arriving in country, while others were hitting the drop date of their DROS.

Since the 365th was considerably larger than the Third Field, the ratio of patrons for the Red Bull was about seventy-five percent aviators to twenty-five percent doctors and nurses. Most of the nurses he recognized, but he saw one that he had not seen before . . . a pretty lieutenant with chestnut hair, high cheekbones, blue eyes, and a shape that no military uniform could hide.

At first, he felt a little guilty for admiring her, but then he remembered that he didn't have anything to feel guilty about. Glenda had divorced him.

There are no encumbrances upon this young warrant's ass, he thought.

The nurse was sitting at the end of the bar and Brandywine stared at her until she looked around. When she did look around, he smiled.

The nurse left her seat and walked over to his table. "May I join you?" she asked.

"Of course," Brandywine replied. "That's why I brought you over here."

The nurse looked confused by his response. "I beg your pardon? How did you bring me over here?"

"By staring at you until the back of your neck started to burn."

The nurse laughed. "You are full of it," she said, but subconsciously, she put her hand to the back of her neck.

"Oh, I don't deny that. But, you did come over, didn't you?"

"It was a coincidence."

"Believe what you want, but I . . . *have the pow -wer.*"

Brandywine was over the top, making two, very distinct syllables out of the word power, rather like a tent revival preacher.

"Oh, you have the power, do you?"

"Absolutely. Why, just ask anyone about me, and they'll tell you. My name is W.W. Brandywine."

"W.W. Brandywine? Oh yes, as a matter of fact, I have heard of you," the nurse replied. "They say you are a manipulator. Are you a manipulator, W?"

Brandywine started to tell her that he preferred to be addressed by his last name, but he hesitated. He liked the way she said W. He liked the smile on her lips as the single letter rolled off her tongue. And, as she was the only one who had ever referred to him in such a fashion, it bespoke a degree of intimacy that he also liked.

"Am I a manipulator? Yes, I suppose I am sometimes, if it serves my purpose. You are new here, aren't you? And by new, I mean, within the last thirty days."

"I've been here two weeks today."

"Only fifty weeks to go," Brandywine said. "What's your name?"

"Lieut . . . " the nurse started, then she stopped and smiled. "That is, Jane," she said. "Jane Grey."

"Jane Grey, huh? Would that be Lady Jane Grey? Can I buy you a drink, Lady Jane Grey? A beer maybe? Or, under the circumstances, perhaps a Bloody Mary would be more appropriate."

Jane applauded softly. "Oh my . . . that's very good. You are the first person since I've arrived here who has made that connection. You know all about Lady Jane Grey and Mary Tudor do you? I am impressed."

"I'm an impressive kind of guy," Brandywine said.

At that moment a captain passed by and upon seeing Brandywine, stopped.

"Well, if it isn't Brandywine, back in country. When did you get back?"

"Today," Brandywine said. He made no effort to introduce Jane.

"I figured sure you would find some way to stay in the States."

Brandywine held up his hand. "I'm not responsible for any money you might have lost by betting on me."

"I didn't bet," Captain Hicks said. "Oh, by the way, I hear you lost your old job. You'll be working for Colonel Cleaver now."

"Yes."

"What does he have you doing? Wait . . . don't tell me. Knowing how he feels about you, he probably has you in charge of all the shit burners in the Saigon Military District."

"I don't know what he has in mind; he hasn't told me."

"Well, whatever it is, you can bet he won't let you get away with all the crap you did before."

"I'm sure I won't."

"So, did you meet with your publisher?"

"I did."

"And for that Colonel Cleaver got you to agree to a six month extension." It wasn't a question; it was a statement of the obvious.

"That's right."

Captain Hicks laughed. "I hope he kissed you when he screwed you like that. W.W. Brandywine, the great wheeler-dealer, getting his clocked cleaned by Colonel Cleaver."

"Wow, is that true?" Jane asked.

"Is what true? You mean about Brandywine getting his clock cleaned?" Hicks asked.

"No . . . I mean, about selling a book." She looked at Brandywine with an expression of interest on her face. "Did you really sell a book?"

"Yes."

"To a New York publisher?"

"Hardcover rights to Pendarrow House, paperback rights to Foster-Crescent."

"What's the title?"

"Brandywine's War," Brandywine said. He smiled. "Uh, the title is a little immodest, I'll admit."

"Wow. Now I really *am* impressed."

"You're impressed; I'm stunned," Hicks said. "I can't believe anyone would buy anything Brandywine would write. Hey, Brandywine, just how much money did you get anyway?"

Brandywine started to tell Hicks that what he got for the book was none of his business. Instead, he just stared at him for a moment.

"Well, I feel pretty good about this," he said. "I know it's hard to believe, but I got less than one-hundred thousand dollars for it."

Captain Hicks looked shocked. "What? One hundred thousand dollars? My God, you got that much? You got less than one-hundred thousand dollars?"

"Yep," Brandywine said, nodding. "I mean, who would've thought that a boy from the little old town of Sikeston, Missouri, would ever get that much money, just for writing a book? But that's what I got all right."

"One hundred thousand dollars! Man, what are you going to do with all that money? Are you going to stay in the Army?"

"Of course I am. I love the Army, and I consider it a noble and honorable profession."

"Man, what I couldn't do with that kind of money."

"Oh, by the way, I ran into Colonel Hedrick while I was at D.A. Has he contacted you yet?"

"Contacted me? Contacted me about what?"

Brandywine shook his head. "I'm not at liberty to tell," he said. "I just know that it's between you and Captain Fender."

"What's between me and Captain Fender?"

"Why, whichever one Colonel Hedrick chooses," Brandywine said.

"Chooses to do what?"

Brandywine shook his head. "I can't tell you," he said. "All I can say is . . . may the best man win."

"The best man win? It's our next assignment, isn't it?"

"I can't say," Brandywine said.

"Can you at least give me a hint?"

"That wouldn't be fair. I didn't give Captain Fender a hint."

"Come on. He's the XO. He doesn't need a hint. He has an unfair advantage over me anyway."

"All right. All I can say is . . .she likes officers to show a little flair."

"Who? What?"

"So, if you are going to have any chance at being her personal pilot . . . you'd better be a bit more flamboyant. Oh, and develop a taste for Greek food. The Vice-President is Greek, you know, and his daughter likes . . . " Brandywine put his hand to his lips. "I've already said too much."

"Damn. Colonel Hedrick is looking for a pilot for Agnew's daughter, isn't he?"

"That's classified. I can't say. And for sure, don't say anything to Captain Fender about it."

Hicks put his finger to his lips and shook his head. "Don't worry; I'm not going to say anything to Fender. More flamboyant, huh?"

"It might help," Brandywine said.

After Hicks left, Jane looked across the table at Brandywine, with a bemused smile on her face.

"W, you are as full of shit as a Christmas goose," she said.

"What gives you that idea?"

"Well, for one thing, you *did* say *less* than one-hundred thousand, didn't you?"

"Yes."

Jane laughed. "What is so funny is that you said one thing, and he heard another. Is there a Colonel Hedrick?"

"I'm sure there is one, somewhere."

"My God. Calling you a manipulator is an understatement. You, Mister Brandywine, are the master."

"And you are as smart as you are pretty, Lady Jane Grey," Brandywine said. "Let's be friends."

At 0900 the next morning, Brandywine returned to the 365th Aviation Battalion Headquarters. He signed the visitors' log before stepping over to Specialist Clark's desk.

"Yes, sir, Mister Brandywine, I see that you're back," Clark said. "What can I do for you?"

"I would like to see Colonel Cleaver," Brandywine said.

Again, Clark checked his book, and again, he shook his head.

"Oh, no, gee, I'm very sorry, Mister Brandywine, but you still don't seem to have an appointment."

"Okay," Brandywine said easily.

"Would you like me to make an appointment for you? It's no problem."

"No, I'm a patient man," Brandywine said. "I'll just wait until the colonel wants to see me."

Clark laughed. "You slay me, Mister Brandywine," he said.

"Have you been to Vung Tau yet?" Brandywine asked Jane over dinner that night.

"No, I haven't."

"Can you get off tomorrow?"

"Gee, I don't know."

"Sure you can. Tell them you have a sick aunt. Tell them you have to deliver a serum to an Eskimo village. Tell them you are carrying General Abrams' love-child and he has asked for a secret meeting."

Jane laughed. "What is so important about getting off tomorrow?

"I'm flying over to Vung Tau. I don't have an assignment yet, so Major Casey asked me to deliver a helicopter there," Brandywine said. "And I have a friend who can bring us back Saturday morning. You really need to go."

"That would be two days off, tomorrow and Saturday."

"Well, yes, but you'll be off Saturday anyway, won't you?"

"I'm supposed to work this Saturday."

"Get someone to cover for you. I promise you, you will enjoy Vung Tau."

Jane drummed her fingers on the table for a moment or two as she studied Brandywine's face.

"You know, my bosses frown on fraternization."

"Oh, hell, they're talking about doctors," Brandywine said. "And you can't blame them for that. I mean, suppose some nurse and some doctor are having an affair, then they break up, and she's all upset about it. Next thing you know they are in surgery together, he asks for a spreader or something, and she jams it right up his ass."

Jane had just taken a drink, and she laughed out loud, spraying Brandywine with beer.

"Damn," Brandywine said, picking up a napkin. "I've only worn this shirt three days; I figured I had at least two more days left."

"It's your own fault," Jane said. "Okay."

"Okay what?" he asked, as he dabbed at his shirt.

"Okay, I'll go with you. What time?"

"I'll meet you right here at ten hundred tomorrow," Brandywine said. "I would be earlier, but I have someplace to be at nine."

Chapter Nine

When Brandywine showed up at 365th Aviation Battalion Headquarters the next morning, he waved at the gardeners, then went inside and signed the visitors' register. He stepped over to Specialist-5 Clark's desk.

Clark wasn't there.

"Where's Clark?"

"He has a dental appointment this morning," a PFC said. "Can I help you, sir?"

"Yes, I'm CW-3 Brandywine . . . here to see Colonel Cleaver."

The PFC looked at the appointment book and shook his head. "I'm sorry, sir, I don't see your name on the appointment book."

"Really? Are you sure? W.W. Brandywine. Look again."

The PFC looked a second time. "Not here, sir."

"Okay, thanks."

"Do you want me to make you an appointment, Mister Brandywine?"

"No . . . that's okay, I'll try again sometime," Brandywine called back over his shoulder.

Brandywine returned to the Red Bull and sat drinking coffee as he waited for Jane, hoping she would be able to get off.

An officer, wearing Stateside greens, stepped up to Brandywine's table.

"Excuse me. Are you an officer?"

"What?" Brandywine replied.

"I mean, I know you are an officer because this is an officers' club," the man said. "Isn't it?"

"Can I do something for you . . . ," Brandywine started, but he halted in mid-sentence because, although the uniform had the striped pants and cuff of an officer, he was wearing neither rank nor branch insignia. "What are you?" Brandywine asked. "You don't have your rank on."

"I don't know what I am," the man answered. "I'm whatever this is."

He held out a little blue box of Myers Insignia. Behind the cellophane were the oak leaves of a major.

"Or, maybe this is my rank," he said, holding out another box. "I can't seem to get it straight."

The second box had a set of caduceus. When Brandywine saw that, he laughed.

"You're a doctor, aren't you?"

"Yes, I'm Doctor Carl Largent."

"That explains it. How long have you been in the Army, Doctor Largent?"

"What's today?"

"Friday."

"Then I have been in for three days. They gave us a briefing when we were sworn in, but all of it went right over my head. I know I'm an officer of some kind, and I know that I outrank some officers, while some outrank me. I don't know what rank I am or what rank you are."

"You see this?" Brandywine said, pointing to the oak leaves. "That means you are a major." Then he pointed to the cloth W-3 bar sewn on his collar. It was in the muted combat colors of black and brown. "This means I am a chief warrant officer. The word chief is all you have to remember. You do know what a chief is, don't you?"

"Well I know what a chief surgeon is. Is it anything like that?"

"Something like that," Brandywine agreed. All the time Brandywine was talking, he was pinning the major's insignia onto Doctor Largent's uniform. "There you go, you're all set. Now, you think you've got this rank business straight?"

"Yes, sir, uh, Chief," the major said. "Look . . . thanks for explaining it to me. I must say that was a lot simpler than all the rigmarole they gave us when we were sworn in. Oh, I forgot. Should I salute you?"

"No, that's not necessary," Brandywine said with

a magnanimous wave of his hand. "We're not all that big on saluting over here."

"Really? Seems to me like they said something about saluting."

"Well, ordinarily that would be the case," Brandywine agreed. "But consider this. The VC could be anywhere. Now, suppose a VC was hiding somewhere, and he saw you salute me. He'd know then that I was a chief, and I'd be a prime target."

"Oh!" Major Largent said. "Yes, of course. I should have realized that. Please forgive me; I really had no intention of putting you in danger."

"Ah, don't worry about it," Brandywine said. At that moment he saw Jane coming into the Red Bull. The expression on her face wasn't happy.

"I can't go," she said.

"Why not?"

"The chief of nurses isn't here today, so I have to have a doctor authorize my absence."

"Any doctor?" Brandywine asked.

Jane nodded. "Any doctor assigned to Third Field," she said.

"No sweat," Brandywine said. He turned to Major Largent. "Carl, wasn't it?" he asked.

"Carl, yes, sir," the major said. "Doctor Carl Largent."

"I tell you what, Carl, I am flying over to Vung Tau today, and it is important that Lieutenant Grey go with me. I wish I could tell you why, but it is classified. How about authorizing her absence?"

"Oh, I don't know if I can do that or not," Major Largent answered, hesitantly. "I haven't even reported in."

"Have you got a set of your orders?" Brandywine asked.

"Yes, sir, right here," Dr. Largent said, pulling them from his inside pocket.

"Let me look at them," Brandywine said.

Largent handed him the packet of orders and Brandywine made a big production of studying them. Taking a pen from his pocket, he put his initials on one of the copies and then printed below the mimeographed orders: *1/LT Grey is hereby authorized to accompany CW-3 W.W. Brandywine on a flight to Vung Tau.*

"Okay," Brandywine said, handing the pen to Dr. Largent. "As you can see, I've initialed the orders, designating that you have arrived. All you have to do is sign this, and that will allow Lieutenant Grey to go with me. Or, if you prefer, you could furnish me with another nurse who is properly trained for this mission."

"Well, I don't know that I could . . . I mea . . . I don't even know what the mission is. What is the mission?"

"I'm sorry, Carl, I can't tell you that. Like I said . . . it is classified. I can tell you that, as far as I know, Lieutenant Grey is the only one who fits all the requirements. Unless, of course, you know of someone else."

"What are the requirements?"

Brandywine shook his head. "Sorry, I can't tell you that either. I'm sure you understand. But, you're the doctor here, so it's your decision to make. Do I take Lieutenant Grey, or do I scrub the mission?"

"Is it an important mission?"

"That depends on whether you are a Republican or a Democrat."

"What?"

"How much importance do you place on President Nixon's health?"

"My God! Is the President coming to . . .?"

"Shh!" Brandywine said, putting his finger to his lips and looking around the club. He held up his finger. "Never discuss classified information in public like that. You have no idea who might be listening, and loose lips sink ships."

"I'm sorry, I had no idea, I . . . " Major Largent halted in mid-sentence, afraid to say anything more, lest he further jeopardize the mission.

"So, it's your call, Doc. You can authorize Lieutenant Grey's absence, or you can scrub the mission. Which will it be?"

"Oh, I think she should go. I definitely think she should go."

"Well, okay, if you really think so," Brandywine said. "Like I said, it's all up to you."

Major Largent signed the copy of the order and Brandywine folded it up and put it in his pocket. He then handed the rest of the sets of orders back to the doctor. He looked over at Jane, who had been following the exchange in open-mouthed shock.

"Lieutenant, we'd better get underway," Brandywine said authoritatively. "I want to pull pitch by ten thirty."

"Are you sure this is all right?" Jane asked somewhat hesitantly. She looked at the doctor.

"Go ahead, Miss . . . uh, I mean, Lieutenant," Dr. Largent said. He put his finger across his own lips. "But, mum's the word. You heard what the Chief said. Loose lips sink ships."

"Okay, thanks."

As Brandywine and Jane started toward the door, Brandywine called back to the doctor.

"Oh, by the way, Carl, I noticed that your orders said report no later than tomorrow. If I were you, I'd take the rest of the day off and just relax. Why don't you take a cyclo downtown and have a look around Saigon. You'd better enjoy yourself while you can. It's going to be a while before you get another chance."

"Okay, Chief, I will," Doctor Largent said. "And thanks."

Outside the club, Brandywine unlocked the padlock and unthreaded the chain that wound through the steering wheel, as Jane climbed into the other seat.

"What was all that business about President Nixon coming to Vung Tau?"

"I didn't say the President was coming to Vung Tau. All I did was ask him how much importance he put on the President's health."

"But you left him with the impression that we were on some sort of mission that had to do with the President."

"Did I? Now I wonder what could have ever given him that idea."

"Yes, I wonder. Well, listen, I'm going to need a change of clothes if I'm going to spend the night in Vung Tau," she said. "So I hope we have time to run by the NBOQ."

"Okay, I'll run you over there, but try not to talk to anyone," Brandywine said as he started the jeep.

"Wait a minute. You aren't telling me that guy we just met isn't really a doctor, are you?"

"No, he's a doctor all right," Brandywine said. He held his hand up and twisted it slightly. "But let's just say that the authorization he just signed could be subject to change if the wrong person looked at it."

Jane laughed. "They were right about you, W. You are a manipulator."

"Brandywine," Captain Hicks said, coming out to the flight line as Brandywine was doing his walk-around inspection. "What do you think?"

Captain Hicks pulled a long white scarf from his pocket and wrapped it around his neck.

"This is pretty flamboyant, don't you think?"

"Well, it's a step in the right direction," Brandywine agreed.

"I need more?"

"If I know Fender, you'll need more."

"But, he doesn't even know about it yet, does he?"

"I don't know. He's pretty resourceful."

"Here he comes now," Hicks said. "I'd better get out of here. I don't want him to know that I know."

Captain Hicks left quickly as Captain Fender approached.

"Major Casey wants these reports to go to Group," he said, handing an envelope to Brandywine.

"All right."

Fender saw Jane sitting in the left front seat of the helicopter.

"Sniff?" he asked.

"Oh, that's Lieutenant Grey," Brandywine said. "Major Largent asked me to take her over to Vung Tau."

"Major Largent?"

"He's a new doctor at Third Field."

"Oh. Well, always glad to help out our friends at Third Field. Sniff, sniff, snit."

"I notice you seem to be using that inhaler a lot," Jane said. "Do you have an allergy?"

"What inhaler? Sniff?"

"That, uh . . ." Jane started to reply, but when she

saw Brandywine shaking his head, she stopped in mid-sentence. "Nothing," she concluded.

"Brandywine, Hicks told Martin that Colonel Hedrick was looking at him for his next assignment," Fender said.

"Damn. He promised me he wouldn't say anything about it."

"You told me that would be my assignment."

"All right, look, I'm not supposed to tell you this, but . . . "

"But you already told Hicks," Fender said with a pout. "Snark!"

"No . . . I didn't tell him this." Brandywine lifted his finger. "Don't tell anybody what I'm about to tell you. Do you promise?"

"Sniff," Fender promised.

"Colonel Hedrick and I are old friends. We served together in Germany and Fort Eustis. So he is counting on me to make the decision as to which one of you he chooses for the job."

"You're to make the decision?"

"Well, not officially of course. Officially, Colonel Hedrick will make the decision. But he will take my suggestion. Showmanship."

"Snert?"

"Just watch Captain Hicks, and follow his lead," Brandywine said. "No, not follow his lead . . . make him follow yours."

"Sniff," Fender said, nodding his head by way of thanks.

"Trapp, stand fireguard. Let's kick the tire and light the fire," Brandywine said as he climbed into the right seat.

Chapter Ten

There were only four people in the helicopter as it beat its way toward Vung Tau. Brandywine was in the pilot's seat, which on the UH1 was the right seat. Jane was in the left seat, Specialist-6 Trapp, the crew chief, and Specialist-5 Dagen, the door gunner, rode at their stations looking out over the M-60 machine guns that were hanging muzzle down on their mounts in the open doors.

"How do you like it so far?" Brandywine asked Jane, through the intercom.

Jane tried to answer, but Brandywine couldn't hear her. "See that switch there on the cyclic? Looks like a trigger?" he said, pointing to it.

Jane nodded.

"Depress it, but only depress it to the first detent.

That will let you talk just to me. If you pull it all the way back, you'll be broadcasting to the whole world."

Jane pulled the switch back to the first detent. "Like this?"

"Yes."

"I like riding in a helicopter," Jane said. "I have to admit . . . this makes me even hornier than straddling a motorcycle."

Startled by her response, Brandywine looked into the back of the helicopter where he saw both the crew chief and the door gunner laughing.

Confused, Jane looked around as well.

"Uh, Lieutenant," Brandywine said, depressing the mike switch. "When I said you would be talking only to me, I meant you would be only inside the helicopter. All of us are on the same feed."

"You mean . . . you mean they heard what I just said?" Jane asked.

"Yes, ma'am, we heard every word," Specialists-6 Trapp replied, laughing.

"Hey, Lieutenant, don't sell motorcycles short. I've got one," Dagen said. "Come see me in Eugene, Oregon, when you get back to the land of the big PX, and I'll be glad to give you a ride."

Jane was mortified for just a moment, but then she joined the others in laughter.

The helicopter Brandywine was flying was one that had been remanded to the 65th Transportation

Company for direct support maintenance. Its maintenance cycle completed, Brandywine was now returning it to its home company, the 58th Air Assault Company, stationed at Vung Tau.

Vung Tau was a busy place, with helicopters as well as fixed wing aircraft, landing and departing. Like every other place in Vietnam it was dusty during the dry season, wet during the monsoon season, and hot all year around.

"Are you guys going to be all right? Do you think you can find a place to stay?" Brandywine asked his crew after he turned over the helicopter and the 780 gear to the maintenance officer of the 58th.

"Find a place to stay in Vung Tau? Are you kidding, Chief?" Trapp replied. "We'll get along just fine. Don't you worry about us."

"I have to worry about you. It's an officer thing, looking out for the welfare of your men and all," Brandywine said. He put the back of his hand against his forehead. "You enlisted men don't know how easy you have it . . . not having to deal with the weight of command."

"Uh, Mister Brandywine, warrant officers don't command. They are technical officers, remember?" Trapp said.

"Really?"

"Really."

"Then you mean I don't have to deal with the weight of command?"

"No, sir," Trapp said, laughing.

"Oh, well then the hell with you. You can both sleep in the street as far as I'm concerned. What a relief."

Trapp and Dagen laughed as they walked away from the helicopter. Jane was waiting just off the flight line and Brandywine walked over to join her.

"I've seen to my men, and they are all squared away," he said. "Now, how about you? Are you ready?"

"Well, I've got my AWOL bag," Jane said. She nodded toward the little overnight bag she had packed. "So what do we do now?"

"Now, we go to The Pacific to get us a room."

"The Pacific?"

"It's a hotel."

"Uh, W, I like you a lot, but I'm not ready to share a hotel room with you."

Brandywine laughed. "No, it's not like that. The Pacific is a hotel, but it has been taken over by the Army and is being used as a BOQ. Nurses stay there too, and it's pretty easy to find an empty bed in one of the rooms. We do it all the time."

"Okay."

"It's off the base, so I'll get the duty driver to run us down there," Brandywine said. "Then, after we get us a bed, we can go down town. They call Vung Tau the 'Riviera of the Orient.' Trust me. You'll like it."

The duty driver had only a three-quarter ton, so

Brandywine helped Jane into the back, and he climbed in after her. The back was covered by a tarp so they watched the base unfold behind them: helicopters squatting on the perforated steel planking that made up the hardstands, jeeps, two-and-a-half ton trucks, hooches, sandbags, shit-burners, guard towers, bunkers, red dirt, and billowing dust. The driver stopped at the gate and the MP on duty looked into the back. Seeing Brandywine and Jane there, he saluted. Brandywine and Jane returned the salute.

"Go ahead," the MP called to the driver, and the truck pulled away, the high-pitched whine of the universal singing as it did so.

When they got to The Pacific, Brandywine saw someone he knew standing in front of the hotel.

"There's Mister Lambdin," he said, nodding toward a warrant officer who was leaning back against the front wall of the building, letting a boy shine his boots. "Ray!" Brandywine called.

"Brandywine, what are you doing over here?"

"I brought one of your birds back," he said. "Listen, do you know anybody with an empty bed for tonight?"

"Well, as it so happens, you can stay with me," Ray said. "My roommate is on R and R right now."

"This is Lieutenant Grey. You think you can find a place for her?" he asked.

Ray smiled at Jane. "Sure, I don't take up that much room," he teased. "You're welcome to share my bed."

"Thanks, but no thanks," Jane replied.

Ray shrugged his shoulders. "It was just a thought. But no problem, I know several of the nurses who billet and mess here, so we can ask around at lunch."

By the time lunch was over, Jane had made arrangements to share a room with a nurse major from Saint Louis. Jane's mother was from Saint Louis, and Jane had been there enough times to know the city, so she and the major were able to make some connections.

After lunch, Brandywine and Jane walked outside where in front of the BOQ they saw more than a dozen cyclos lined up along the curb, waiting for customers. There were two kinds: those that were human powered and those that were engine powered. Both were similar in that they had a bench seat in front with the driver sitting high behind.

The drivers of the pedal-powered cyclos were shirtless and wore shorts. Their thin, dark legs were knotted with muscles and scarred from a lifetime of mosquito bites and various injuries. The motor-cyclo drivers wore long pants and free flowing shirts. All wore conical straw hats.

The area along the curb where they were parked reeked with the stench of noxious fumes that billowed up from the loud, two-cycle engines. One of the drivers, seeing Brandywine and Jane, called out to them.

"Want cyclo?"

"How much?"

"Five hundred P."

"Fifty Piasters," Brandywine countered.

"You dinky dau . . . you say fifty P. I do for four hundred P."

"Seventy-five P."

"You cheap-shit GI! Three hundred P."

"Seventy-five P."

The driver twisted the throttle a couple of times causing the engine to roar and the smoke to pour.

"Two hundred P," the driver said.

"No, I see someone over here who just said he would do it for one hundred P," Brandywine said, starting toward one of the other drivers.

"You no say one hundred P," the driver said quickly. "You say one hundred P . . . I do."

"Okay, you've got a deal," Brandywine said. "Get in," he said to Jane.

"I've never ridden in one of these."

"You are in for a treat."

As soon as Brandywine and Jane were in the seat, they were off with a neck-snapping start. The first thing Jane noticed about the cyclo was that they were not only the passengers, but they were the bumper as well. Their driver came screaming down on the back of a truck at breakneck speed, stopping at the last minute with a protesting squeal of tire against pavement. More than once they stopped so close to a big truck that Jane could have reached up to touch it.

Finally, they reached the middle of town where the cyclo driver pulled across in front of oncoming traffic without so much as a signal. Jane gasped as another cyclo whizzed by. The odd thing was that neither cyclo driver gave the slightest notice of the other.

"Well, that was invigorating, don't you think?" Brandywine asked, as he paid the driver.

"Invigorating?" Jane asked. "It was terrifying."

With the transaction completed, the cyclo driver roared off in a cloud of blue smoke.

Chapter Eleven

Brandywine and Jane wandered around Vung Tau all afternoon, winding up at a place called the Blue Diamond for dinner.

"Is it all right to eat here?" Jane asked as they went inside.

"Are you kidding? This is a great restaurant. And they've got a patio out on the roof that overlooks the water."

"I don't know. I've just heard so much about health conditions and all."

"No, no . . .they weren't talking about restaurants; they were talking about vi dokey . . . that's all," Brandywine said with a dismissive wave of his hand.

"Vi dokey?"

"Yeah, you know, VD, clap, syph, that sort of thing. When they have those big health lectures, that's what they are talking about. I've never heard them say don't eat spring rolls or soup."

"I don't recall any lectures about . . . what did you call it? Vi dokey?"

"Yeah, well, officers don't have to worry about the vi dokey anyway. We never get the clap . . . don't you know that?"

"No, I didn't know that."

"Nope, never. We do, sometimes, get non-specific urethritis."

Jane laughed. "I must've missed that class in nurse's training."

"Unless I miss my guess, he'll be out on the patio," Brandywine said as he pushed through the crowded dining room.

"Who will be out on the patio?"

"My best friend in the entire world."

When Brandywine stepped out onto the roof patio, he saw B. Dowling Mudd, sitting alone, at a table in the far corner. A single beer bottle sat in front of him, and he was busy writing.

"There he is . . . writing to his wife," Brandywine said, pointing.

"How do you know he's writing to his wife?"

"How do I know? Well, because his hand is moving and there is a pen in it," Brandywine said. "Come on. I want you to meet him."

Brandywine led Jane across the patio. B. Dowling Mudd didn't look up until Brandywine reached his table.

"Brandywine!" he said, standing quickly and sticking out his hand. "I'm so glad you came back."

"To hell with the handshake, B. Dowling Mudd. I want a kiss!" Brandywine said, putting his arms around his friend.

"What?" B. Dowling Mudd asked, twisting uncomfortably to get away.

"Come on, B. Dowling Mudd. I promise. No tongue. Just a nice, warm kiss on the lips between two men."

Brandywine puckered his lips and B. Dowling Mudd turned his head away.

"Stop that!"

"Okay, I'll just kiss you on your manly chest," Brandywine said as he began unbuttoning B. Dowling Mudd's shirt.

"What has gotten into you? Have you gone crazy?" B. Dowling Mudd asked, pushing Brandywine away.

"All right . . . all right. I know it embarrasses you to kiss me in public. We'll wait until we are alone somewhere," Brandywine said. He threw his arms out and stepped back. "I'm breaking clean, see? No contact . . . no contact."

"You are crazy," B. Dowling Mudd said. He began to button his shirt in an attempt to recover some decorum.

"B. Dowling Mudd, I want you to meet my new friend and current lover, Lady Jane Grey," Brandywine said, introducing Jane.

Seeing Jane, B. Dowling Mudd came to attention and saluted.

"It is a pleasure meeting you, Lieutenant," he said.

Jane looked at Brandywine. "Is he serious?"

"You'd better return his salute, Lady Jane, or he will hold it until hell freezes over. And in case you haven't noticed it, we are already in hell, and it isn't likely to freeze over anytime soon."

Self-consciously, Jane returned B. Dowling Mudd's salute. B. Dowling Mudd brought his hand down sharply, but remained at attention.

"Tell him as you were," Brandywine said.

"What?"

"Tell him as you were. B. Dowling Mudd is the most soldierly soldier you will ever meet in your life. He does everything according to the FM-22-5."

"What is the FM-22-5?"

"Tell her what FM-22-5 is, B. Dowling Mudd."

"It is the Army Field Manual for Drill and Ceremonies, Ma'am."

"We had to learn it in pre-flight," Brandywine said. "Most of us just learn it, but B. Dowling Mudd memorized it. B. Dowling Mudd, what is the position of attention?"

B. Dowling Mudd began speaking in a steady, monotone.

"To assume the position of attention, bring the heels together sharply on line, with the toes pointing out equally, forming an angle of 45 degrees. Rest the weight of the body evenly on the heels and balls of both feet. Keep the legs straight without locking the knees. Hold the body erect with the hips level, chest lifted and arched, and the shoulders square. Keep the head erect and face straight to the front with the chin drawn in so that alignment of the head and neck is vertical. Let the arms hang straight without stiffness. Curl the fingers so that the tips of the thumbs are alongside and touching the first joint of the forefingers. Keep the thumbs straight along the seams of the trouser leg with the first joint of the fingers touching the trousers. Remain silent and do not move unless otherwise directed. Ma'am," he concluded.

"My God, is he for real?"

"He's for real," Brandywine said. "Now, tell him as you were. Otherwise he will hold that position until he retires from the Army."

"As you were."

B. Dowling Mudd relaxed. "Thank you, ma'am," he said.

Brandywine and Jane joined B. Dowling Mudd for supper, Jane deferring to Brandywine to order for her.

"*Bhan trang couon tom, bon hung dam, ga xoi mo, and bun mae,*" Brandywine ordered. "*Oh, and nuoc nam. Lots of nuoc nam.*"

"Wow, that's very good," Jane said. "Now, what will we be eating?"

"Spring rolls, beef fondue, and sort of a bar-b-que chicken, with baguettes of bread, with a side of fermented fish-sauce," Brandywine said. "And it is good."

"I'll have a hamburger and French fries," B. Dowling Mudd told the waiter. "Mayonnaise on the hamburger . . . ketchup with the French fries."

"Hamburger and French fries? In a restaurant like this, why would anyone order a hamburger and French fries?" Jane asked.

"B. Dowling Mudd is afraid that if he eats anything un-American, he could lose control of his will power. And if he did that, why the next thing you know he would be buying Saigon Tea for the bargirls and getting drunk while off duty. Why, he might even become a Democrat."

"Never," B. Dowling Mudd responded. "I would never do anything like that."

Jane looked over toward the patio bar and saw several very pretty and sensuously dressed Vietnamese girls, talking and flirting with the American soldiers. She pointed toward the bar.

"Mister Mudd," she started, but Brandywine interrupted her.

"You can't call him that," he said.

"I beg your pardon?"

"The name Mudd cannot stand alone."

"What are you talking about?"

"You know . . . like oxygen can't stand alone? It is a diatomic molecule always expressed as O2. B. Dowling Mudd's name is like that. It is never simply Mudd, nor even Mister Mudd. It is always B. Dowling Mudd."

"Okay," Jane said. "Mister B. Dowling Mudd, many of those girls are very pretty. Do you mean to tell me that in all the time you have been in Vietnam you have never had anything to do with any of them?"

"I've never had anything to do with any of them," B. Dowling Mudd said.

"He's not lying," Brandywine said.

Jane smiled. "And you have never voted for a Democrat?"

"No ma'am," B. Dowling Mudd said, and this time his answer was even more resolute than it was before.

"I told you," Brandywine said. "B. Dowling Mudd is what Shakespeare would call 'a prince of a fellow.'"

"I've never met a prince before," Jane said. She leaned over and planted a quick kiss on B. Dowling Mudd's cheek.

"Lieutenant!" B. Dowling Mudd gasped. He put his hand to his cheek and wiped, as if wiping away the kiss. "I'm a married man!"

"Hell, Lady Jane, you've never even kissed me," Brandywine said, surprised by the action. "What'd you kiss him for?"

"I wanted to see if this prince would turn into a frog," she said, laughing.

Chapter Twelve

After dinner the three walked through the soft, warm night air, stopping occasionally to look at some of the items being sold by aggressive street vendors. The merchandise displayed on the small stands ran the gamut from hats, to jewelry, to military insignia.

"W, would you look at this? I can't believe it," Jane said, picking up a watch from a table. "This says this is a Rolex."

"You betcha ass this be numbah one Rolex," the vendor said.

"Let me see it," Brandywine said. He held the watch up to his mouth and bit down on it.

"What you do? You clazy GI . . . you dinky dau!"

"It tastes like a Rolex," Brandywine said, handing the watch back to Jane.

"How much?" Jane asked.

"Two thousand P."

"Twenty dollars?" Jane gasped. "Twenty dollars for a Rolex?"

"You thinkee that two much? One thousand five hundred P."

"You can beat that," Brandywine said. "You can get it for ten dollars."

Jane put it down. "Wow, ten dollars. Too bad it isn't a lady's Rolex."

"No sweat," Brandywine answered. "It isn't a man's Rolex either."

Jane laughed. "Really," she said sarcastically. "And after you made such a big deal about it tasting like a Rolex."

"Rolex? Did I say Rolex? I meant to say it tasted like a Timex." He stuck his tongue out and wiggled it a couple of times. "You know the kind that takes a licking but keeps on ticking?"

Shortly after Brandywine, Jane, and B. Dowling Mudd walked away from the vendor's stand, they were accosted by a Vietnamese boy. He was about twelve, wearing a pair of khaki pants and a T-shirt that said Mickey Mouse.

"GI's you want girl?" he asked. "She very good girl. Almost a virgin . . . you like very much."

"Just one girl?" Brandywine asked.

"Brandywine," B. Dowling Mudd cautioned.

"My sister, yes. Just one girl."

"But there are three of us," Brandywine said. "If

she does all three, she won't be almost a virgin anymore, will she?"

"Wait a minute here, W! What do you mean three of us?" Jane asked.

"*Choi ong!*" the young pimp said. "You want girl for girl?"

"Do I want a girl for her? Hell no. Let her get her own girl," Brandywine said.

"W!" Jane said, hitting Brandywine on the shoulder, but ameliorating it with laughter.

When they went into the "Pretty Girl and Happy GI Bar," Brandywine saw Ray Lambdin sitting with a girl at the table in the back. The jukebox was playing Neil Diamond's "Sweet Caroline."

"Hey, there's Ray," Brandywine said. "Let's go talk to him."

"He looks busy," Jane suggested.

"Ah, she's just trying to get him to buy her a Saigon Tea. Or, in this case, a Vung Tau Tea. Come on. We'll run her off and save him some money. Trust me; he'll thank us for it."

The three went back to the table and stood there for a moment. The bar girl looked up with a big smile, but when she saw Jane, the smile faded.

"*Choi oi!* What you do? You bring your own girl?" she asked.

"Yes, and she can whip your ass, so you'd better go," Brandywine said. "*Di di.* Oh, and bring us four beers."

The girl left and Brandywine and the others sat down.

"Damn, and here I thought she was just beginning to like me," Ray said. "Hello, B. Dowling Mudd."

"Hello, Ray," B. Dowling Mudd said.

"You mean it is true? Everyone really does call him B. Dowling Mudd?" Jane asked.

"Even his mama," Brandywine said.

The bar girl returned with four beers, and B. Dowling Mudd started to pay for it but Brandywine held out his hand. "Let Jane pay for this round," he said.

"Why me?" Jane asked.

"Don't you want to be one of the boys?"

"No, I don't want to be one of the boys. If I wanted to be one of the boys, I would've taken the young pimp's offer of his sister."

"Oh, yeah, I guess you would've at that, wouldn't you?"

"But, I will pay for this round," she said as she took the money from her billfold.

"Ray, you met Lady Jane Grey earlier today, but did I tell you she was my fiancée?"

Jane, who by now was beginning to understand Brandywine, smiled over Brandywine's fiancée remark.

"Oh, so you are going to get married, are you?"

"Yeah, well, I don't have any choice," Brandywine said, taking a large swallow of beer. "She tricked me into it. She's pregnant."

Jane's smile broadened.

"How long have you two known each other?"

"Three days now," Brandywine said.

"Oh, well then, that explains why she doesn't look pregnant."

"She's not showing yet. But soon we won't be able to keep our secret from the rest of the world, will we, dear?"

"Brandywine, that type of fraternization between the ranks is totally unauthorized," B. Dowling Mudd said disapprovingly.

"Hey, since when does love let a little thing like the difference between a warrant and commissioned officer get in the way?" Brandywine asked.

"Sweet Caroline" recycled on the jukebox.

"Did you three know each other before you came to Vietnam?" Jane asked.

"B. Dowling Mudd and I went through flight school together," Brandywine said, "and all three of us were in Germany together."

"I've heard Germany is a good tour."

"It's a great tour," Ray said. "B. Dowling Mudd and I had our wives with us while we were there."

At the mention of wives, Jane's eyes narrowed, and, as if just considering the possibility, she turned to Brandywine.

"How about you, W? Was your wife there?"

"I married my wife there," Brandywine answered easily.

"Oh?" Jane replied with an arched eyebrow.

"And I divorced her in Newport News, Virginia," he added.

"You and Glenda are divorced?" Ray asked. "When did that happen?"

"About three weeks ago, while I was home on leave," Brandywine said.

"I'm sorry to hear that."

"Yeah," Brandywine said. "Well, it was her choice, so there wasn't much I could do about it." Then a smile spread across his face. "On the other hand, it is true what they say about rebound. With Lady Jane, it was love at first sight."

"Tell me . . . has he always been this . . . this unrestrained?" Jane asked.

"Are you kidding?" Ray asked. "You are seeing his subdued side."

Jane laughed.

"Do you know that when I arrived in Germany, Ray met me at the *Eisenbahnhof* with a fifty dollar bill," Brandywine said. "Now, how can you not like a guy like that?"

"I figured if he was anything like me, he had been in transit for a while, so it had to be at least a month since he had been paid," Ray said.

"He figured right," Brandywine said. He chuckled. "I rode that damn train from Frankfurt to Schweinfurt, which is a hell of a long trip I want to remind everyone, without a bite to eat because I was stone, cold broke."

"So, how did you repay me for my kindness?" Ray asked. "By making me feel like a heel when I commented on how you walk."

"Commented? It was an outright insult," Brandywine said.

"What are you talking about?" Jane asked.

"Don't tell me you haven't noticed the way Brandywine walks," Ray said.

"Yes, it's called slew foot."

"Slew foot?"

"He turns his feet outward as he walks."

"Notice how much nicer her observation is than yours," Brandywine said.

"I saw him walking across the flight line one day," Ray said, "and I told him that I thought he walked like a damn duck."

"I told him, yes, I know that," Brandywine said. "And then I asked him if he knew why I walked like that."

"Of course, I said I didn't," Ray said.

"When I was nine, I was in a terrible car accident," Brandywine said. "My sister and my aunt were both killed, and I was so badly injured that the doctors said I would never walk again."

"Oh, W," Jane said. "How terrible."

"Yes, it was awful. But, I was determined that I would walk again, so sometimes in the middle of the night, I would get out of the hospital bed and walk as far as I could. Often I would pass out in the hall of the hospital and the nurses would have to pick me up and carry me back to my room.

"I kept working at it until I could walk with crutches, then with canes, and finally with no help at all. Yes, I know I walk funny, but I am just thankful that I can walk at all."

"Oh, no, W, you don't walk funny. You . . . you should be proud of what you accomplished."

"See! See! She fell for it too!" Ray said.

"Fell for it?"

Brandywine chuckled, as he took a swallow of his beer.

"It's all a lie," he said. "I just walk funny."

"Oh, you!" Jane said, laughing, as she hit him on the shoulder. On the jukebox, "Sweet Caroline" started playing for the third time, and Jane looked toward it.

"Wow," she said. "I had no idea that song was that popular."

"What song?"

"That song. 'Sweet Caroline.'"

"Oh, yeah, well, I don't even notice it anymore," Ray said. "The reason it is playing so much is because it is the only song on the jukebox."

"It is a good song."

"Yeah, but it isn't *the* song," Brandywine said.

"What is *the* song?" Jane asked.

"The one about going to San Francisco with flowers in your hair."

Ray and B. Dowling Mudd laughed, but Jane saw something in Brandywine's eyes.

"You know . . . for anyone else over here, a warrior like you, I would think they might be teasing. But not you. I think you are serious."

"I am serious," Brandywine said.

"Well, what the hell do you like about that song?" Ray asked. "As far as I can tell, it's just a song about a bunch of damn hippie freaks with flowers in their hair."

"Yes," Brandywine said, "but, I find that concept strangely . . . appealing."

"You are a complex man, W," Jane said.

"Some call me complex . . .some call me screwed up," Brandywine said in an attempt at humor, his way of keeping anyone from getting too close.

"And you, Mister B. Dowling Mudd, are the strong silent type. You are awfully quiet," Jane said.

"He's always quiet. He doesn't approve of this, you know," Brandywine said.

"Doesn't approve of what?"

"Hanging out in bars . . . boozing it up and being with women."

"Being with women?" Jane asked. "What women? I don't see any women here."

"Well, hell . . . you're a woman, aren't you? I mean, you made a big point earlier about not being one of the boys."

"Well, yes, but I'm a benign woman. I mean, even if I'm not one of the boys, I'm one of the boys."

The three men looked at each other.

"I think that was one of those woman things," Brandywine explained. "Sometimes their brain sort of opens onto another dimension, and I think we have just been a witness to that."

"No, I mean . . ." Jane started, and then she dismissed the subject with a wave of her hand. "Never mind. Is that right, B. Dowling Mudd? You don't approve? Not even of me?"

"It's not just you, Lieutenant. I don't approve of being in any bar with any women, anywhere."

"And yet, here you are," Jane said.

"Yes, here he is, but he only comes to places like this to keep me out of trouble," Brandywine said. "Ever since I appointed him my best friend, he has taken on the obligation to look out for me. Isn't that right, B. Dowling Mudd?"

"Yes."

"Where are you from, Mister B. Dowling Mudd?" Jane asked.

"From?"

"Where were you born?"

"He wasn't born. He was issued on a DD Form 1348," Ray said.

"I was born in the hospital at Fort Riley," B. Dowling Mudd said. "My father was in the Army."

"Tell her where your father was born?"

"He was born in the hospital at Fort Riley."

"So you are third generation Army?"

"Fourth generation," B. Dowling Mudd said. "My great grandfather served with Custer."

"When we were in the Seventh Cavalry back in Germany, B. Dowling Mudd was the only one in the entire squadron who had a relative who had fought with Custer," Brandywine said.

"I thought everyone who was with Custer died."

"No, ma'am. My great grandfather was the ferrier sergeant for Captain Weir's company."

"Tell her where your two kids were born," Brandywine said.

"Let me guess," Jane said. "Fort Riley?"

"One was born at Fort Benning, and one was born at Fort Rucker," B. Dowling Mudd said.

"Oh, what a shame to break up such a nice streak," Jane said.

"You do know that it's marked on B. Dowling Mudd's medical records that he can't give blood, don't you?" Brandywine asked.

"He can't give blood? Why not?"

"Because what flows through his veins isn't blood. It is a combination of horse piss, gun oil, hydraulic fluid, and jet fuel."

The others laughed. Then Ray looked at his watch. "Hey, they are showing a movie on the roof of the Pacific tonight. If we hurry back, we can see it."

"What is it?"

"*Romeo and Juliet.*"

"*Romeo and Juliet?*" Brandywine scoffed.

"Shakespeare's *Romeo and Juliet*? Are you serious? Who would want to see that?"

"Oh, that's the Franco Zeffirelli version isn't it? I'd love to see that movie!" Jane said.

"Yeah, me too," Brandywine said, changing his tone quickly. "Okay, let's go."

"Sweet Caroline" was playing on the jukebox as they left the bar.

Chapter Thirteen

Outside the Blue Diamond, they flagged down one of the little blue and yellow Renault taxis.

"You dinky dau, not all can fit in taxi," the driver said, when he saw there were four of them.

"No sweat, can do," Brandywine said. "Lambdin, you ride in the front seat; B. Dowling Mudd, you can ride in the back with Lady Jane and me."

"There's not room for three of us in that little back seat," B. Dowling Mudd said.

"Sure there is. Lady Jane can ride in my lap. But, before we start, I want to caution you against trying to cop any feels."

"I would never try and take unfair advantage of a woman like that," B. Dowling Mudd said, indignantly.

"I wasn't talking to you, B. Dowling Mudd. I was cautioning Lady Jane about putting her hands on me."

The four managed to squeeze into the car. Laughing, they started back to The Pacific hotel.

When they reached the hotel, they went up onto the roof to watch the movie. All during the movie, the horizon to the north and west kept flashing with light, followed by a deep rumble.

"Oh, I hope the rain doesn't come before the movie is over," Jane said.

"What rain?" Brandywine asked.

"Haven't you been seeing the lightning and hearing the thunder?"

Brandywine, Ray, and even B. Dowling Mudd chuckled.

"What's so funny?"

"That isn't lightning," Brandywine said. "It's artillery fire.

"Oh."

After the movie, Brandywine walked Jane to her room. She was still wiping away the tears.

"Come on, who cries at a movie? I mean, *Romeo and Juliet*? It's not like you didn't know how it was going to turn out. It wasn't all that sad."

"It was too," Jane said. She smiled. "You can't hide it; I saw your eyes glistening a little."

"It was the cigarette smoke."

"Yeah, sure, of course it was. W, I want to thank you for asking me to come to Vung Tau with you," she said when they reached the door to the room where she would be staying. "I have had a wonderful time today. You have no idea how much I needed this."

"Yeah, I do know how much you need it," Brandywine said. "When you consider that you see every day what most of us see only occasionally, you have it rougher than any of us."

Brandywine put his thumb and forefinger under her chin and lifted her head toward his.

"You owe me," he said.

"What do I owe you?"

"I'll think of something." He moved his lips down to hers. The kiss was gentle at first, and then she warmed to it, leaned into him, wound her arms around his neck, and opened her mouth on his. The kiss was long and deep and then they broke it off.

Jane smiled up at him. "Whoa, did you just give me tongue?" she asked. "And here, I thought you told B. Dowling Mudd you didn't do tongue."

"It depends on who is the tongue-er and who is the tongue-ee," Brandywine said with a chuckle.

Ray Lambdin was sitting at his desk writing a letter. Brandywine let himself into the room.

"You still up? I thought you'd be in bed by now."

"I was just finishing this letter," he said. "Did you enjoy the movie?"

"Well, I would've picked something a little more

cheerful," Brandywine said. "But, yes, I enjoyed it all right."

"I probably wouldn't have watched it, but Janet saw it and told me not to miss it."

"How are Janet and the kids?"

"They're doing great," Ray said. He laughed. "Johnny has made himself a short-timer stick, and he carries it to school with him now. He is counting down every day until I come home."

"How many days do you have left?"

"Thirty-seven days," he said. "I've already got my orders. I'm going to Fort Eustis."

"Ahh, my old stomping ground. I'll probably be coming back there too when this tour is over," Brandywine said as he turned down the blanket and sheet and crawled into bed. "That is if this tour ever ends. Colonel Cleaver made me extend for six months."

"Yes, B. Dowling Mudd told me about it. It was because of your book, wasn't it?"

"Yeah. Damn, Ray, just think. I'm going to be published. Who would've thought it?"

"I always thought it," Lambdin said. "You wrote that little Christmas play back in Germany, remember?"

"Yeah, but that was just for kids."

"Yeah, but I know kids, and I know that the kids really enjoyed that play. It was very good." Lambdin turned off the desk lamp, and except for the ambient light from outside, the room grew dark. Through the window, could be seen the flashes of distant artillery.

"You don't have to quit writing just because I'm going to bed."

"I was finished. I'm ready to go to bed, too. I've got a flight tomorrow."

"Where you going?"

"I'm taking a generator to an A-team at Dak Tho."

Ray went to bed as well, and the two lay there in the dark talking.

"You know what I think is the hardest thing about being in Vietnam?" Ray asked. "Other than being away from your family, I mean."

"For me, it's trying to find a water cooler somewhere that has water instead of Kool-Aid," Brandywine said.

Ray chuckled. "No . . . I mean, other than that."

"What?"

"It's getting over the fear that every time you go out, you could get killed."

"Yeah, you got that right."

"Do you ever worry about getting killed?"

Brandywine waited for a moment before he answered. "Sometimes I guess I do," he admitted. "But generally, it's before a mission. I don't seem to worry about it once the mission starts."

"What about after the mission is over?"

"No, I know some guys do but I figure . . . after it's all over, what's there to worry about?"

Ray chuckled. "Yeah, that's the way I feel about it too." There was another long pause. "What do you think happens?"

"What?"

"When you die, I mean. What do you think happens? Do you think you know it? I mean, like, okay, you're dead. Now, in the next instant is your soul still here, sort of looking around, trying to figure out what happened?"

"I don't know. But let me ask you. If your soul survives, and you can be anywhere you want to be, do you intend to hang around here in Vietnam?"

"Ha!" Ray said. "I won't be waiting for DROS, orders, transportation or anything. My ass is going to be out of here."

"You mean your soul's ass, don't you?" Brandywine asked, and the two men shared another laugh.

"You aren't a religious man, are you, Brandywine?"

"I don't know; it depends on what you mean by religious," Brandywine answered.

"Well, I mean, like go to church regularly. I'm Catholic, so there's never been any question about me going to church. How about you?"

Brandywine chuckled. "When I was a private at Fort Rucker, I used to go into Ozark to go to church. Part of it was because I thought I *should* go to church, and part of it was because it seemed like a good place to meet girls. Also, some family would always invite you over for a Sunday dinner of fried chicken.

"But, I got into an argument with the preacher once over a theological question that I really was interested in. When he couldn't answer it, he pointed a bony finger toward the door and told me to get out. 'Get out of my church and don't come back until you are right with God,' is the way he put it."

"He had no right to do that," Ray said. "He had no right to call it 'his' church."

"I know. But that was a tall order. I mean, telling me not to come back until I was right with God. How do you ever know if you are right with God?"

"I guess you just have to know," Ray said.

"Look, Ray, I believe. I mean, I'm not an atheist or anything like that. But I guess I just haven't convinced myself yet that I am right with God."

"Do you pray?"

"Yeah," Brandywine admitted. "Before every flight."

"Yeah, me too," Ray said.

Chapter Fourteen

The next morning Brandywine, Jane, and B. Dowling Mudd rode down to the flight line with Ray Lambdin. Trapp and Dagen were already standing by the helicopter they would be taking back to the 65th.

Ray's helicopter was there as well, and his crew chief and door gunner were talking to Brandywine's crew. Seeing Brandywine, Ray's crew chief, a powerfully-built black man, came over and saluted. "Good morning, Mister Brandywine."

"Hello, Huler. Lieutenant Grey, this is Emerson Huler. He worked for me when we were at Fort Eustis. He's also a pretty good football player. He played for Rip Engle at Penn State. Tell her what position you played, Huler."

Huler smiled. "I played the rest of the team," he said.

"I beg your pardon?" Jane asked, confused by his answer.

"I played the rest of the team," Huler said. "You know how they always introduce the starters one at a time and let them run onto the field . . . then they say, 'and the rest of the Penn State team.' That's when I would run out onto the field screaming like crazy."

Jane laughed.

"Don't let him fool you, Lieutenant," Brandywine said. "I remember the 1962 Gator Bowl game when Penn State played Florida. I saw that game on TV. Penn State lost to Florida, seventeen to seven, but if it hadn't been for Huler, they would've lost by at least two touchdowns more. Huler was in their backfield all day."

Huler laughed. "I only made one tackle for the whole game, but thanks for building me up, Chief."

"That's okay," Brandywine said. "Bragging on someone doesn't cost anything. It's not like I'm lending you money."

Huler laughed again. "I'd better get over there. Looks like Mr. Lambdin is doing his pre-flight."

"Are we topped off, Specialist Trapp?" B. Dowling Mudd asked.

"Yes, sir, all fueled and ready to go," Trapp replied.

A WO-1 came running up the flight line.

"Where you been, Dan?" Ray asked. "I thought we were going to have to take off without you."

"Sorry I'm late," he said. "I just now found out I was scheduled."

"That's my friend, Brandywine," Ray said, as he twisted the tail rotor back and forth, checking the pitch-change links. "Introduce yourself."

"Dan Morris," the WO-1 said.

"I'm Brandywine; this is my live-in lover, Lady Jane Grey."

"Lady Jane? You mean, like royalty?" Morris asked.

"She's Queen Elizabeth's second cousin, twice removed," Brandywine said. "Of course, there's a little thing like the U.S. Constitution that says she can't use her title in America, but I say royalty is royalty. Don't you agree?"

"Oh, yes," Morris said. "Yes, I do agree."

"Of course, the Queen doesn't approve of her sleeping with a commoner like me. That's why she had to join the Army."

"How long have you two been . . . uh . . . I mean, well . . .?"

"You want to know how long we have been sleeping together . . . is that it? Go ahead . . . you can ask it. We aren't shy, are we dear? Well, it all started in summer camp when we were sixteen. The girl's camp was just on the other side of . . ."

"Morris, get your ass over here before he completely warps your mind," Ray called.

"Yes, sir," Morris said.

Brandywine shook his head as Morris hurried over to Ray's helicopter. "Damn, that kid is so young and gullible it takes all the fun out of teasing him. I wonder if he has a permission slip from his mama to be over here."

"Don't be mean to him," Jane said. "I think he's cute."

"Cute? Cute?" Brandywine slapped his hands over his heart. "I'm hurt . . . truly hurt."

Since B. Dowling Mudd would be pilot in command on the way back, he did the walk-around for his helicopter at the same time Ray was doing his own pre-flight. A few minutes later everyone was on board and both helicopters started their engines at about the same time.

Brandywine could hear the igniters popping through the earphones of his helmet, and he watched the instruments as they stabilized. Then, from the other helicopter, he heard Ray call the tower.

"Vung Tau, this is Top Tiger Four at the maintenance pad . . . ready for take off."

Almost immediately afterward, B. Dowling Mudd called.

"Vung Tau, Good Nature Three at the maintenance pad . . . ready for take-off."

"Winds are out of the east at ten knots, altimeter is two niner, niner eight. Top Tiger, cleared for immediate departure over antennae farm. Good Nature, hold."

"Top Tiger, up," Ray said, and Brandywine glanced across to wave at his friend as the other helicopter lifted from the pad and began climbing out.

"Good Nature Three, you are cleared for immediate take off. Follow Top Tiger over the antennae farm. Contact Paris Control for firing coordinates."

"Good Nature Three, up" Brandywine acknowledged for B. Dowling Mudd.

As soon as they departed, Brandywine switched over to Paris Control. "Paris Control, Good Nature Three departing Vung Tau, two thousand feet, on a heading of two-seven-five."

"Good Nature Three, squawk your parrot," Paris Control said.

Brandywine pulled a toggle switch on the transponder.

"Roger . . . Good Nature Three . . . we have you."

Paris Control then began giving firing coordinates, indicating what artillery operations were in progress, where the shells would impact, and their perigee, thus allowing them to avoid collision.

Half way back they saw a fire mission in operation, and turning in his seat, Brandywine pointed it out to Jane. They could see the muzzle flashes of the American artillery and several seconds later the detonation of the shells on target.

Jane enjoyed watching the spectacle, recalling the firing from last night. Then, she realized that there were people under those explosions. Enemy soldiers, yes, but people nevertheless, and she felt a little queasy at being able to watch from such a remote position.

The flight back to the 65th was about half-an-hour in duration and when they returned, Brandywine borrowed B. Dowling Mudd's jeep to take Jane back to her quarters.

"Whenever you go to San Francisco," Jane sang on the way back to the NBOC. "You really do like that song, don't you?"

"Yeah."

"I think you would look cute with flowers in your hair." She took off his cap and ran her fingers through his very closely cropped hair. "That is . . . if you had any hair," she added with a chuckle.

"I should have never mentioned that."

"No, I'm glad you did."

"Why?"

"I'm just . . . glad you did," she said. "I enjoyed the weekend."

Brandywine smiled. "I'll see if we can't have a few more. Oh, and when you see Major Largent, tell him President Nixon is doing fine."

Jane laughed. "I'll do that," she promised.

When Brandywine returned to the flight line, he saw Major Casey standing in front of the hangar.

"Mister Brandywine, did you report to Colonel Cleaver?"

"I reported to Battalion, yes, sir," Brandywine said, avoiding the information that he had not yet actually seen Colonel Cleaver. He pulled four pieces of chewing gum foil from his pocket and handed it to Casey.

"Thanks," Casey said. "Listen, you don't have any idea of what's going on between Captain Fender and Captain Hicks do you?"

"Going on? What do you mean?"

"I think they're losing their minds. Now Hicks is going around smoking a corncob pipe and wearing a scarf and hat like General Macarthur. And Captain Fender is wearing jodhpurs and knee-high leather boots."

"Well, you have to admit . . . they always have been a little odd," Brandywine said.

"That's true. Oh, has Colonel Cleaver given you your new assignment yet?"

"No, not yet," Brandywine said. "Why do you ask?"

"Captain Martin has received his orders. He's going home this week and nobody has been assigned to take over the open storage depot. That would be a good assignment for you. The TO&E calls for a captain, but I think you could handle it."

"Yeah, I would like that assignment," Brandywine said.

"Well, don't let Colonel Cleaver know you would like it. The way he feels about you, the last thing he wants to do is give you anything you might actually want."

"Yeah, I guess you're right."

Lieutenant Kirby stepped out of the recovery office then, carrying his flight helmet. There was a big smile on his face.

"We got one," he said.

"Got one what?" Casey asked.

"A recovery mission. And it's just the kind I've been looking for. Not on some LZ, but a single recovery out in the boonies." He held up his index finger. "This is the kind of mission that can earn a DFC."

"Where is it?"

"It's at Dak Tho. A helicopter was delivering a generator to an A-team up there, and he got shot down."

"Oh, shit. Was it a Top Tiger?" Brandywine asked.

"Yes, how'd you know?"

"Damn. I know the pilot. Where is B. Dowling Mudd?"

"He's back at the hooch taking a shower," Kirby said. "I'm about to send Trapp to get him."

"No, don't bother him," Brandywine said.

"What do you mean . . . don't bother him? We've got a recovery," Kirby said.

"Major Casey, request permission to make this recovery," Brandywine said.

"Sure, go ahead," Casey replied.

"Major Casey, I'm in charge here and I . . .," Kirby started, but Casey interrupted him.

"You're in charge? Well now, that's funny, Lieutenant. And here, all this time I thought I was C.O."

"Well, yes, sir, you are," Kirby said dissembling. "But I just . . ."

"Brandywine is going with you," Casey said, interrupting.

"Yes sir."

"Thank you," Brandywine said to Major Casey.

"Be careful up there," Casey said as he started back toward the orderly room. As he walked away he pulled the little strips of tinfoil from his pocket and began playing with them.

"You do understand, don't you, Mister Brandywine, that I will be in command during this flight?"

"Yeah," Brandywine said. "I understand. Now get your ass in gear and let's go."

Chapter Fifteen

"There's Dak Tho," Brandywine said as they circled around a little village. "But I don't see the helicopter. I'm going to switch to the ground push."

". . . read me, over? Helicopter circling Dak Tho, do you read me?" Brandywine heard as soon as he switched to the FM frequency.

"This is Good Nature Three, we read," Brandywine said. "Are you our ground security?"

"Roger, Good Nature Three, Bayonet One, here."

"Pop green smoke, Bayonet One," Kirby said.

"No!" Brandywine shouted, but it was too late. A column of green smoke started curling up from beneath the jungle canopy.

"There they are," Kirby said, turning toward the column.

"Oh. And just which one do you think is them?" Brandywine asked.

"What?"

Brandywine pointed to three other columns of green smoke.

"If we pick the wrong one, we're toast," Brandywine said.

"Oh, shit. I didn't think."

"That's all right, Kirby. Don't worry about it. You're a lieutenant. No one expects you to think." Brandywine came up on the FM push again. "Bayonet One, pop smoke, I'll verify."

"Will do."

A column for rose-colored smoke began curling up. "Uh, I've got red."

"That's affirmative."

Kirby started toward the smoke. So far he had not made that good an impression on Brandywine, but Brandywine had to admit that the kid could fly. He sat them down smoothly in an area that had very little blade clearance.

That was when Brandywine saw the helicopter, or what was left of it. It didn't look good.

Kirby killed the engine.

"Dagen, get up here and pull my chicken plate back," Brandywine said.

The chicken plate Brandywine was referring to was the sheet of armor that was on the side of Brandywine's seat. It slid forward between him and the door, and while it did provide protection from small arms fire, it made it impossible for the pilot and co-pilot to get out without assistance. For that reason, pilots and co-pilots often found that they had to smash through the chin bubble to escape crashed aircraft.

Dagen pulled the plate back, and even before the blades stopped spinning, Brandywine was out of the ship, heading toward the lieutenant in charge of the security platoon.

"I'm Lieutenant Bates," the platoon leader said.

"I'm Mister Brandywine. Has Dust Off been here yet?"

"Dust Off?"

"To rescue the crew."

The lieutenant shook his head. "Nobody to rescue, Chief," he said. "They're all dead."

"Where are they?"

"Well, the door gunners are lying out on the ground. We were able to get them out. But the pilot and co-pilot are still inside. They're wedged in so tight we couldn't get to them. I figured you might have the equipment to do that."

Brandywine walked over to the downed helicopter. It was a twisted, mangled, unrecognizable pile of aluminum. The nose of the helicopter was thrust under an elevated tree root and though Brandywine could see the bodies, they were so mangled that it looked like they were part of the wreckage.

A paperback book was on the floor in the back of the helicopter, amazingly undamaged. The pages riffled in the wind, and then it blew closed. The book was *The Carpetbaggers*, by Harold Robbins.

"Holy shit, how are we going to get this thing out of here?" Kirby asked coming up then.

"We aren't," Brandywine said.

"What do you mean we aren't? We came out here to recover this helicopter. We're taking it back."

"Come on, Kirby," Brandywine said. "How are you going to lift it out? Not only is the lift link busted, the whole thing is: mast, transmission, everything. This isn't a helicopter; this is a scrap heap."

"Have you seen them like this before?"

"Yes."

"What do you do when they're like this?"

"We'll take the data plate and burn the rest."

"What about the KIAs?"

"They aren't KIAs, Kirby; they are people." He pointed to the one in the right seat. "That is Ray Lambdin. His wife's name is Janet. He has two kids: Johnny, who is one heck of a pitcher on the little league team in Canton, Mississippi, and Karen, who is going to grow up to be a beautiful young woman. The co-pilot is Warrant Officer One Dan Morris. Morris is here by mistake. His mama thought she was giving him permission to go to summer camp . . . he wound up here.

"The crew chief is Specialist Huler. Huler knew

more about the hydraulics system of the UH-1 than anyone I know. He used to teach a six-hour block, without ever referring to a note, and he got everything right. He was also a pretty good football player.

"I didn't know the door-gunner. But I can promise you that someone knows him, and back in the States, his mother is probably watching Johnny Carson right now, with maybe just a little worry in the back of her mind, but at this very moment, falsely content in the belief that her son is still alive.

"No, Lieutenant, they aren't KIAs."

"I'm sorry, Chief, I didn't mean for it to come out quite like that," Kirby said.

Brandywine sighed and gave a little dismissive wave of his hand.

"I know you didn't, Lieutenant," he said. "And I apologize for coming down so hard on you." He pinched the bridge of his nose. "It's just that I'm going on three years in this God-forsaken place now, and the shit just gets deeper."

"I understand," Kirby said.

"No, you don't," Brandywine said. "Not yet, anyway. Come back and talk to me after you've been here for ten months or so. Then you will understand." Brandywine looked over at Trapp, who was examining the Wreckage. "Trapp?"

"Yes, sir?"

"Get whatever tools you need and get them out. Then toss in a thermite grenade."

"Yes, sir," Trapp said. "I think that's about the only thing we can do. Uh , what do we do with the bodies once we get them out?"

"Lieutenant Bates, you got any body bags back in the ville?" Brandywine asked the security platoon leader.

"We brought some with us."

"Good. We'll bag 'em and take 'em back."

"They aren't from our unit," Kirby said.

"We're taking them back, Lieutenant," Brandywine said.

"All right, all right. I was just pointing out that they weren't from our unit; that's all."

For the next several minutes the jungle reverberated with the sound of a power saw and wrenching metal. Brandywine walked back over to the helicopter and sat in the open door, not particularly wanting to see Ray when they pulled him out. Kirby, on the other hand, showed an almost morbid interest in it, until the bodies were pulled out and then he turned away. A moment later, Brandywine saw the lieutenant throwing up.

"Mister Brandywine, we've got 'em all bagged up," Trapp said. "What now?"

"I'm not in charge," Brandywine said. "He is." He nodded toward Kirby, who was leaning against a tree, his face almost as green as the leaves.

"Come on, Mister Brandywine. He doesn't know whether to shit or wind his watch, you know that."

"Make sure the ammo chutes are clear; then burn it."

"Yes sir."

The four dead Americans were brought back to the helicopter and put in the back. Because they were in body bags, Brandywine didn't know who was who, and he was glad.

"Fire in the hole!" Trapp shouted. His shout was followed by a popping sound. Within minutes, what was left of the helicopter was a burning inferno.

Suddenly, there was the sound of shooting, and for a moment Brandywine thought they were being attacked. Kirby thought so as well, because he came running by Brandywine and dived into a depression just behind the helicopter.

Brandywine then realized that it was just rounds cooking off. It stopped after about three more rounds.

"Trapp, I thought I told you to clear the chutes," Brandywine said.

"Sorry, sir," Trapp said. "Those must have fallen under the floor plating.

Kirby, realizing now that the gunfire was cooking ammo and not enemy fire, stood up and began brushing himself off.

"Shit!" he said. "Ouch!"

"What is it?"

"I jumped into a thicket of thorns. I've got

scratches all over me," he said as he pulled an imbedded thorn from his forearm.

"*Chieu hoi*," someone said from the ditch behind the helicopter. "*Chieu hoi*."

"Lieutenant Bates," Kirby said, irritably, calling to the security platoon leader as he began picking out the thorns. "One of your ARVNS is over here."

"ARVN hell," Lieutenant Bates replied. "That's a VC."

"VC?" Kirby said, jumping away.

The VC put up his hands. "*Chieu hoi?*" he said again.

"What the hell is he saying?"

Lieutenant Bates laughed. "He's surrendering."

"Surrendering?"

"*Chieu Hoi*. Surrender," the VC said.

Kirby made a clawing grab for his pistol. Pulling it, he pointed it at the VC. "Get your hands up," he ordered.

"Hell, Lieutenant, his hands *is* up," Dagen said, laughing out loud.

"Looks like you've got yourself a prisoner, Lieutenant Bates," Brandywine said.

"The hell he does," Kirby said. "I captured him. He's my prisoner, and we're taking him back."

"You can't be serious, Lieutenant," Brandywine said. "How the hell are we going to take him back? We don't have any facilities to deal with a prisoner."

"I am in command here," Kirby said, "and I say we are taking him back."

"Lieutenant Bates, will you take this prisoner off

our hands?" Brandywine called, appealing to the infantry lieutenant.

"Look I've only got an A team. You'd be doing me a favor if you did take him back," Bates said. "The VC hit the ville the other night, and they killed eight villagers including a couple of kids. I think if I took this guy back, the people there would kill him."

"What the hell," Brandywine said. "All right you," he said to the VC. "Get in."

The VC nodded and under the watchful eye of Kirby climbed into the back of the helicopter.

"Your arm is bleeding there, L T. Better let me put a band-aid on it," Dagen suggested as he pulled the chicken plate forward beside Kirby.

"It'll be all right," Kirby replied as he flipped on the battery switch.

With the bodies all loaded and the rigging crew aboard, Kirby started the engine and they took off.

"Dagen," Kirby said as they reached altitude. "Are you keeping an eye on my prisoner back there?"

"How'm I goin' to do that, Lieutenant? I don't have a hand gun."

"Brandywine, you've got the controls," Kirby said.

"I've got it," Brandywine said, wrapping his hands around the cyclic and collective.

Kirby turned in his seat, pulled out his pistol, and seeing that Dagen was too far away handed the gun to the VC prisoner.

"You," he said, pointing at the prisoner. "Give the gun to him." He pointed to Dagen.

"Holy shit, Lieutenant! What are you doing?" Dagen shouted, coming forward quickly to grab the pistol away from the VC.

The VC just smiled.

Chapter Sixteen

When Brandywine stepped into 365th Battalion Headquarters Monday morning, he was carrying a little sack. He dropped the sack on Clark's desk.

"Good morning, Clark," he said.

"Good morning, Mister Brandywine. Oh, what's this?"

"I stopped by the PX and picked up a couple of doughnuts," Brandywine said. "I thought you might enjoy them with your coffee."

"Yes, sir!" Clark said. "Thank you, sir." Clark checked the appointment book. "Oh," he said, looking up. "You still don't have an appointment, sir."

"I don't?"

"No, sir. Uh . . . " Clark slid the sack of doughnuts back across the desk, though he looked at it longingly. "Sir, you aren't trying to bribe me into sneaking you in to see the colonel, are you? Because that wouldn't be right."

"Specialist Clark, are you accusing me of an attempted bribe?" Brandywine asked, sharply. "Do I need to remind you that I am an officer in the United States Army?"

"No, no sir, nothing like that," Clark said.

"I just thought you might enjoy a couple of doughnuts, that's all. But if I was wrong . . ." Brandywine reached for the sack.

"No, sir, you weren't wrong," Clark said quickly, reaching out to pull the sack back. "That was very generous of you, sir."

"I'll just sign the visitor's register and be on my way."

"Mister Brandywine, do you want me to make an appointment for you? I'm sure I can get you in tomorrow."

"No, I told you. I am a patient man. I'll wait until Colonel Cleaver wants to see me."

"All right, sir. Whatever you say."

"Hello, Mister Mot, Mister Phat," Brandywine said to the two gardeners as he got into the jeep.

"Good morning Mister Blandywine," Mot replied as the two Vietnamese civilian gardeners saluted him in greeting.

Leaving Battalion, Brandywine drove back onto Tan San Nhut and then over to the aviation depot open storage.

The 65th Aviation Depot Open Storage was

located at the end of runway three-six so that aircraft were constantly passing overhead, from the F4 Phantom Jets, to the C-130s, to the Vietnamese Air Line's DC-6s, and the "Freedom Birds" of Pan Am, Braniff and TWA that were taking the troops who had completed their tours, back home.

The Aviation Depot Open Storage occupied an area of about two and a half acres, completely enclosed with a very high barbed wire fence. Inside the enclosure were row upon row of aircraft repair parts, from rotor blades, to engines, to transmissions. All the parts were in their original packing containers, and those packing containers were further enclosed in plywood boxes.

A guard stepped out from the gate as Brandywine approached. He saluted and waved Brandywine through.

The open storage area was alive with activity, from forklifts moving large containers around to the "recoupage" operation, which meant building or repairing the plywood crates. Brandywine noticed an exceptionally large number of civilians, both American and Vietnamese.

The headquarters, a small shack, appropriately enough, built of plywood, was in the middle of the yard. Brandywine parked in front of the building and went inside. The air conditioner was very efficient, and it was pleasantly cool.

A young light-skinned black sergeant, sitting at a

desk just inside, was flirting with the Vietnamese secretary. He looked around as Brandywine came in.

"Yes, sir," he said. "May I help you?"

"Is Captain Martin in?"

"No sir, he's busy clearing post. He's going home in two days."

"Who are you?" Brandywine asked.

"I'm Sergeant McKay, sir."

"Sergeant McKay, I'm Mister Brandywine. I'm going to be the new officer in charge."

McKay looked surprised. "You are, sir?"

"Yes," Brandywine said. He smiled at the pretty, young, Vietnamese secretary. "Who are you?"

"I am Miss Ling."

"It's good to meet you, Miss Ling. I'm sure we are going to work well together."

"What about Lieutenant Stewart?" McKay asked.

"Who is Lieutenant Stewart?"

"He's the guy who came in this morning and said he was going to be the officer in charge."

"Damn, that could be a problem, couldn't it?" Brandywine said.

"Sir?"

"Let me ask you this, Mack. Did you like him?"

"Well, sure . . . I mean, he's an officer and all," McKay said.

"Mack, did you like the son of a bitch? Or are you just saying that because he is an officer?"

McKay laughed. "Well, sir, to tell the truth, I

didn't like him all that much. First thing he said was that I was going to have to move my desk out into an empty Conex container. Have you been inside an empty Conex container? It's like a furnace in one of those things."

"Yes, I imagine it would be. Why did he want you to do that?"

"I guess he wanted a bigger office for himself."

"Well, let me ask you this, Mack. If I let you keep your desk in here, would you rather have me as your OIC or Lieutenant Stewart?"

"Well, hell yes, sir. There's not even a question about that."

"I would rather have you too," Miss Ling said.

"Oh? Why is that?"

"I think you are nicer man."

"That's just what she's tellin' you, Chief. Actually, I think she's got the hots for me and wants to keep me around the office."

"You dinky dau!" Ling said, though there was laughter in her voice.

"Then it is settled. You would both rather have me than Lieutenant Stewart."

"Yes sir!" McKay said enthusiastically.

"Good. Then you can help me come up with a way to get Stewart out and me in."

McKay looked at Brandywine for a long moment, the confusion obvious in his face. Then he held up his index finger and cocked his head.

"Wait a minute, Chief; are you saying that you aren't really the new OIC?"

"Well, I don't know," Brandywine said. "It depends on whether or not you know anyone in Thirty-fourth Group personnel."

"Sir, I don't know any officers there . . . " McKay started, but Brandywine waved him aside.

"Mack, have you ever seen an officer actually type out a set of orders and run them through the mimeograph machine?"

"No sir."

"Who does that?"

"Well, mostly the clerks and . . . " McKay stopped in mid-sentence then smiled broadly. "I think I see what you mean."

"Tell you what. You get that taken care of," Brandywine said, "and next Saturday you can invite anyone you want to the champagne breakfast."

"The champagne breakfast? What champagne breakfast?"

"The champagne breakfast we are going to have every Saturday morning for as long as I am OIC."

"I'll make some calls," Mack said, reaching for the phone. "Oh, where are you now? Will we have to cut orders to get you detached?"

"Right now I'm awaiting assignment," Brandywine said.

By that very afternoon, Sergeant McKay

presented Brandywine with a set of orders, assigning him as Officer in Charge of the Open Storage Depot.

"I called Cap'n Martin; he'll be here in about half-an-hour to sign everything over to you," McKay said.

"What about Lieutenant Stewart?"

"We took care of him, too," McKay said. "This time tomorrow morning Lieutenant Stewart will be in Ben Hoa keeping track of entrenching tools."

"You're a good man, Mack."

"Yes, sir. I hope you remember that."

Every morning for the rest of that week Brandywine showed up at the 365th Aviation Battalion Headquarters to sign the visitor's roster. By then he had become such a regular that some of the people in the office actually thought that he worked there.

"Mister Brandywine, I wonder if I could ask you something," a Specialist-4 said as Brandywine stood at the little shelf just inside the door, signing the visitors' register.

"Sure," Brandywine said.

"Would it be all right if we turned that back room into a rec room for the E-fours and below? You know, maybe put in a ping-pong table, and a few card tables or something? I mean, the officers and the NCOs all have a place to go, but we don't."

"What's that room being used for now?"

"Nothing," the specialist replied. "Well, it was going to be an extra room for the colonel in case he ever had to work all night or something. But it's never been used for that, and it's just going to waste."

"Sure," Brandywine said. "Go ahead, fix it up anyway you want."

"Thanks!" the specialist said happily.

"Only, do it this Sunday when nobody is around so you don't disturb the work."

"Yes, sir," the specialist said.

"Mister Brandywine," Clark called. "Aren't you going to ask to meet with the colonel?"

"Oh, yeah, I guess so," Brandywine said. He walked over to Clark's desk. "I would like to see Colonel Cleaver."

Clark made an elaborate show of checking the appointment book.

"Gee, I'm sorry, sir," he said, shaking his head. "I don't seem to have an appointment for you."

Brandywine breathed a sigh of relief. "For a moment there, Clark, you had me . . . "

"Scared?" Clark asked.

"Wondering," Brandywine replied.

The others laughed.

"See you tomorrow at o-nine-hundred, sir," Clark called to him as he left. Brandywine tossed a wave over his shoulder.

On Saturday morning, Brandywine waited just outside the Red Bull until several of the nurses came for breakfast. When Jane saw him, she excused herself from the others then walked over to join him.

"Have you had breakfast yet?" she asked.

"No."

"Well, then we can share a table."

"We can do more than that," Brandywine said.

"What do you mean?"

"You said you wanted to see where I work, didn't you?"

"Yes."

"Come with me."

"Before breakfast?"

Brandywine smiled and shook his head. "Not before breakfast," he said mysteriously. "For breakfast."

The desks in the open storage headquarters shack had been put into position to serve as a base for a long table, made from two sheets of plywood. The result was a sixteen foot long platform filled with breakfast viand, from scrambled eggs with cheese and mushrooms, to SOS, biscuits, bacon, sausage and cereal, as well as several Vietnamese delicacies, all tended by Miss Ling and a half dozen of the young Vietnamese women who worked in open storage.

In one corner of the room was an empty engine container filled with ice; from it protruded several champagne bottles.

Approximately two dozen soldiers milled about and McKay called "at ease," when Brandywine and Jane came in.

"As you were, as you were," Brandywine said. "Carry on. Mack, nobody is eating?"

"I wouldn't let 'em eat, Chief, till you got here," Mack said.

Brandywine walked over to the ice chest, pulled out a champagne bottle, and began working the cork up with his thumbs. After a moment, there was a loud pop, and then champagne spewed from the neck. Brandywine held the bottle up over his head.

"I'm here!" he shouted. "Let the eating begin!"

There were cheers and laughter as the men hurried to fill their plates with food.

"So, what do you think?" Brandywine asked Jane, as he poured a glass of champagne for her.

Jane shook her head slowly and smiled up at him. "W, I have to say that I have never met anyone quite like you."

"Hey!" Mack shouted above the din. "Let's hear it for the chief. Hip, hip!"

"Hooray!"

"Hip hip!"

"Hooray!"

"Hip hip!"

"Hooray," the men shouted again.

"Damn," Mack said laughing. "You know, I saw that in a movie once, and I've always wanted to do it."

Chapter Seventeen

Brandywine, now driving a jeep marked 65th Open Storage, stopped in the circle drive in front of the 365th Aviation Battalion. Before going inside, he walked over to talk to the two Vietnamese gardeners.

"Mister Mot, Mister Phat, how are you? *Chao ong. Ong manh gioi cho?*" he repeated in Vietnamese.

Mot and Phat smiled, showing teeth blackened by years of chewing betel nut.

"*Toi manh nhu thuong,*" Mot said.

"I am fine too," Phat said.

Brandywine handed them each a pair of work gloves. "Here," he said. "It will help keep away blisters."

"*Cam on ong,*" Mot said.

"Thank you," Phat repeated.

"*Khong co gi,*" Brandywine said with a slight nod of his head. He started toward the front of the building, but Phat called out to him.

"Mister Blandeewine."

Brandywine turned. "Yes?"

"You here to see Colonel Creaver?"

"Uh . . . well . . . yes, you might say that."

"You wait," Phat said. "Not go in now."

"What?"

"Colonel leave right now. You stand here, he no see.

Brandywine glanced around and saw a staff car pulling away from under the portico on the side of the house. Colonel Cleaver was riding in the back seat. Brandywine turned his back toward the car so that he wouldn't be recognized. He waited until it had passed through the gate.

"Is okay, now," Phat said. "Colonel Creaver gone. You can go see him."

Brandywine laughed. "Thanks," he said.

As Brandywine stood at the little shelf just inside the front door signing the visitors' register, Specialist Clark came over to speak to him.

"Mister Brandywine, there are some R and R requests on your desk," he said. "Would you sign them before you leave so I can get them processed?"

"On my desk?"

Clark pointed to a desk in the far corner. "That's your desk, sir."

Brandywine looked confused. "How did I get a desk here?"

"I gave it to you," Clark said.

"You did?"

"Well, you are the morale officer and . . ."

"Wait a minute. How did I become the morale officer?"

"Didn't you authorize our break room?"

"Well, yes, but that doesn't . . ."

"Mister Brandywine, look around this room," Clark said.

Brandywine did. There were six men in the room: one Staff-Sergeant, one Specialist-5, three Specialist-4s, and a PFC. All of them looked up at him as he perused the room.

"We work for Colonel Cleaver. If ever anyone needed a moral officer, it is us."

"Clark, I'd love to help you but . . ."

"Mister Brandywine, the only one in this entire headquarters who doesn't know what you are doing is Colonel Cleaver. Haven't you wondered why none of us has put your name on the appointment list?"

Brandywine chuckled. "Yeah, I guess I have," he said.

"You might be interested in knowing that Colonel Cleaver has filed charges against you for failure to repair."

"Oh, damn; that's not good, is it?"

Clark shook his head. "Don't worry. That's Sergeant O'Leary's job. And it hasn't left his desk."

"Hi ya, Chief," Sergeant O'Leary said with a little wave. Brandywine nodded his head.

"See, the way we figure it is you scratch our back, and we'll scratch yours," Clark said.

"Sergeant O'Leary, you are the NCOIC," Brandywine said. "Are you in on this?"

"Yes, sir," Sergeant O'Leary replied. "We all are." He took in the rest of the office with a broad wave of his hand.

"That's blackmail," Brandywine said, "and if all of you are in on it, it might also be considered sedition."

"It might be," Clark said, "but, sedition against who? You or Colonel Cleaver?"

"Son of a bitch," Brandywine said, laughing. "I can see right now that we need to be allies."

"I thought you might figure it that way. So, how about the R and R requests? Will you sign them?"

"Of course I will," Brandywine said.

"Men!" Clark called out. "Meet our new morale officer!"

Everyone in the office stood at attention.

"At ease, men," Brandywine said with a broad smile. "And, as our Navy colleagues say, 'I'm glad to be aboard.'"

When Brandywine returned to the depot, Sergeant McKay greeted him with a Coke. "We've got us a little problem, Chief," he said.

Brandywine punched holes in the top of the can

and raised it to his lips quickly to suck away some of the foam raised as a result of the drink being at room temperature.

"What's the problem?"

"It's Mr. Capp."

"Capp? You mean the civilian fork-lift driver?"

"Yes, sir. He's toked out again this morning. I found him sitting on the forklift on the nod. Last week, he punched a hole in the side of a rotor-blade box, ruining the blade. That's several thousand dollars worth of damage."

"You want me to talk to him?"

McKay nodded. "Yes, sir, I guess so," he said. "But to tell you the truth, I don't know that it will do any good. Captain Martin talked to him several times, but Capp is a civilian, so it didn't seem to make any difference."

"Get him in here and let me try," Brandywine said.

"Okay, sir, if you say so," McKay said without a lot of enthusiasm.

While McKay summoned Capp, Brandywine sat at his desk and drank his Coke while he looked through the paperwork that was in front of him.

"Mr. Capp is numbah ten," Miss Ling said. "The girls say he sometime try to do bad things."

"Well, we'll just see what we can do about him," Brandywine said.

"I think no can do much. He not in the Army. He not work for the Army," Miss Ling said.

A few minutes later McKay returned leading a sullen civilian.

"Mister Brandywine wants to talk to you," McKay said.

"What do you want, Brandywine?" Capp asked in a belligerent tone.

"Is that how you talked to Captain Martin?"

"I can talk to you asshole officers anyway I want," Capp said. "I'm not in the Army."

"No, you're not."

"So, what do you want? I'm busy."

"Do you have trouble with drugs, Mr. Capp?"

"Whether I do or don't, it's none of your business," Capp said.

"I don't agree with you. I believe it is my business. You see, I'm in charge of the depot, so everything that goes on here is my business. And I'm told that your work is not only below par but is sometimes destructive."

"Accidents happen."

"Why are you here, Capp?"

"What do you mean, why am I here? You sent your sergeant to get me."

"No . . . I mean, why are you in Vietnam?"

Capp laughed. "That's an easy one to answer. I'm drivin' a fork lift and making four times more money here than I could back home."

"What you are saying then is it is all a matter of money, right? You don't have any feeling of patriotism or duty or honor or anything like that."

"Get real, you dumb shit," Capp said.

"Capp, I understand that Captain Martin spoke with you about your attitude."

"Yeah, a few times."

"But it didn't do any good, did it?"

"Look, I'll tell you like I told Captain Martin. I don't work for you. I don't work for the Army. I don't even work for the U.S. Government. I work for RMK."

"That's what I thought. You're fired, Capp."

"Ha!" Capp said, laughing out loud. "You can't fire me, dumbass. What part of 'I don't work for you,' do you not understand? You can't fire me."

"Mack, where can I find Capp's supervisor?"

"He's in the RMK office up in Ben Hoa."

"Get him on the phone for me, would you?"

"It's not going to do you any good to talk to Mr. Phillips," Capp said. "Martin already tried it, and Phillips reminded him that I work for RMK, not the Army." Capp took out a cigarette and started to light it.

"Capp, I don't allow smoking in my office," Brandywine said. Capp looked over at the ashtray on McKay's desk, where a cigarette sat burning.

"He's smoking."

"That's his office."

"He's on the line, Chief," McKay said.

Brandywine picked up the phone. "Mister Phillips, this is Chief Warrant Officer Brandywine from the 65th Aviation Open Storage Depot. I thought you might be interested in knowing that I just fired Mr. Capp."

There was a sigh from the other end. "Mister Brandywine, you are new in that position, aren't you? Just took over the open storage. . . when. . . a few weeks ago?"

"That's right."

"I went through all this with Captain Martin, but since you are new, I will now tell you. If you have a problem with Mr. Capp, you refer him to me, and I will take care of it. He works for me, not you. You cannot discipline him, and you certainly cannot fire him."

"Oh, well, maybe you didn't hear what I just said. I said I just fired him."

"You cannot fire him," Phillips said in a louder and more resolute voice. "You have no authority over my men."

"Okay, Mr. Phillips, have it your way. I can't fire him."

Capp smiled, and shifted his weight from one foot to another. "I told you, you couldn't fire me, you dumb shit," he said.

"But, Mister Phillips, let me tell you what I can do. I am in charge of the depot. There is a high fence around the depot, and barbed wire on top of the fence. The only way in to this depot is through the gate, and I have two armed guards standing at that gate, monitoring every one who comes in. Those guards are in the Army, and they work for me, Mister Phillips. Now, as soon as I hang up this phone, I'm going to have Capp escorted out of my depot area. And then I am going to tell my guards that if this low-assed, doped-out, piss-complexioned son of a bitch tries to come back in, they are to shoot him on sight."

"What?" Phillips gasped.

"You heard me, Mister Phillips. I'm kicking his ass out of my depot, and I will not let him come back in, for any reason."

"Well, where will he go?" Phillips asked in a sputtering voice.

"That's not my problem, Mister Phillips. Now, if RMK wants to pay Capp for spending the entire day in a bar in downtown Saigon, why that's not my problem either. Just understand this. Capp will never set foot in my depot again."

There was a long beat of silence from the other end of the phone.

"Are you still there, Mister Phillips?"

"Mister Brandywine, would you put Capp on the phone please?" Phillips replied. This time his voice was much less belligerent.

"He wants to talk to you," Brandywine said to Capp.

"I told you," Capp said, his smile even broader and more arrogant now. He reached for the phone Brandywine was holding, but Brandywine pulled it away from him. He pointed to the one on Miss Ling's desk.

"Use that one," Brandywine said, as he kept this one to his ear.

Capp picked it up.

"Mister Phillips, I told this dumb . . ." Capp started, but that was as far as he got before Phillips interrupted him.

"You're fired," Phillips said.

"What? Look here, you can't . . ."

Brandywine heard a click from the other end, indicating that Phillips had hung up the phone.

Capp stared at the receiver for a moment, as if shocked by what had just happened.

"Sergeant McKay," Brandywine said.

"Yes, sir?"

"Escort this . . . civilian . . . off U.S. Army property."

"Yes, sir!" McKay said with a broad smile.

"Wait a minute," Capp said. "What just happened?"

"What just happened is the Chief just fired your sorry ass," McKay said, laughing.

Chapter Eighteen

The nine men belonged to the First Infantry
Division. Put in by helicopters earlier in the day, they
had secured the area and were now on perimeter
patrol. So far the patrol had been as uneventful as the
insertion. The VC had either never been there or had
faded away when the Big Red One was inserted.

"Hey, Billy, how much longer you got?" PFC
Cooper called.

"Are you kidding? Four days from now, I'll be
cruisin' down Kentucky Avenue, trollin' for some
fluff," Billy answered. PFC William R. Pepper, from
Paducah, Kentucky, was walking point.

"Have you ever thought what might happen if
Charlie got into the records and screwed them all up

so that nobody knew when anyone's DROS was?" Cooper asked.

"I'd kill him if he did that to me," one of the other soldiers replied.

The others laughed. "Hell, Vinnie, that's what we're supposed to be doing anyway is kill Charley, whether he screws around with the records or not," Billy said.

"Yeah, but I mean, I would really kill him," Vinnie replied. "I mean, when you think about it, what are we really fighting for? We're fighting for DROS, R and R, and payday."

"Not me," Billy said.

"Yeah? What are you fighting for?" Vinnie asked.

"A twenty-two-foot jumper at the buzzer, root beer floats, cruisin' in a red '58 Impala convertible and screwin' on the beach."

"Ha, do you think Custer's men were fighting for that shit when my people kicked his ass?" Whitehorse asked. Whitehorse was a full-blooded Sioux who sometimes lamented the fact that he had come over to the enemy's side by joining the U.S. Army.

"Nah, Custer's men didn't even know about basketball then. Didn't have Impala convertibles, either," Billy said.

"Maybe not, but they had beaches, and they sure as hell had screwin'," Vinnie said.

"Hey, Billy, you ever screwed on the beach?" Cooper asked.

"It depends."

"Depends? What do you mean it depends? You either have screwed on the beach, or you haven't."

"Well, I've screwed on the banks of the Ohio River," Billy said. "I have hit a twenty-two foot jumper at the buzzer, I've cruised in my '58 Impala convertible, and I've sure as hell had root beer floats."

"Man, oh man, wouldn't a cold piece of pie and a hot piece of ass go good right now?" Vinnie asked.

"Will you men knock it off and pay attention to what you're doing?" Sergeant Mays said. "The way you're laughing and bullshitting, you'd think you were back in the States."

"Hell, this is like bein' back in the States, Sarge," Vinnie said. "We could be back in Manhattan walkin' down Lexington Avenue for all the Charleys we've seen. I'll bet there ain't none for ten miles in any direction."

Almost as if punctuating Vinnie's comment, the mortar round came in then. There was no whistling or rushing sound . . .just a sudden, totally unexpected, flat, stomach-jarring explosion.

Vinnie was blown apart by the blast. Billy and one other soldier went down.

"Get down! Get down!" Sergeant Mays shouted. "Anyone see where that came from?"

"Over there, Sergeant. I see 'em!" Whitehorse yelled, pointing toward an open area.

Two Vietnamese dressed in black were trying to

make it across the open area and into the trees. As one of them was carrying a mortar tube and the other the base plate, it left no doubt as to their responsibility for what had just happened.

The six remaining Americans opened up on them, all of them firing their M-16s in full automatic mode. Under the hail of fire, both VC went down.

"Cease fire, cease fire!" Sergeant Mays shouted. "You're wasting ammo."

After the last echo died, the silence was broken only by the call of a distant bird.

"Johnny, you're the closest. Check 'em out," Sergeant Mays called.

Running bent-over, Specialist-4 John Mayfield moved to check on the three men.

"How are they?" Sergeant Mays called.

"It looks like they're dead," Johnny called back.

"All three of 'em?"

"Yeah, all three."

"I'm not dead," Billy said, his voice so weak as to barely be audible.

"Shit! He's alive! Sarge, Billy's still alive!"

Johnny looked at Billy's wounds. The lower half of his left arm was gone. So was the lower half of his left leg.

"Oh, shit, oh, shit," Johnny said. "I've got to stop the bleeding. Yeah, stop the bleeding."

Johnny took the compression bandage from Billy's belt and started applying it to the stub of Billy's arm.

By now Sergeant Mays and Whitehorse had come over as well.

"Whitehorse, get the compression bandages from Vinnie and Pete," Sergeant Mays said. "They won't be needing them. And get their boot strings; we need a couple of tourniquets."

"All right, Sarge," Whitehorse said.

"Cooper," Sergeant Mays shouted. "Call Six. Tell 'im we've been hit and we need Dust Off!"

Cooper began talking into the little hand-held radio.

"Vexation Six, Vexation Six, this is Rover Two, over!"

"This is Vexation Six, go ahead."

"We been hit! Three men down, two dead, one badly wounded! Get Dust Off in here!"

"And tell 'em to send us a medic," Sergeant Mays shouted.

"Also, we need a medic. Now!"

"Roger, we're sending out reinforcements and a medic," Vexation Six replied. "Dust Off has been called."

"They're on their way, Sarge," Cooper said.

"You men keep a sharp lookout," Sergeant Mays said as he applied the tourniquet. "There's only six of us right now, and that's leaving our ass sort of hanging out here."

Within five minutes after Cooper called the

company commander, the reinforcement platoon arrived with a medic. The medic relieved Sergeant Mays, applied disinfectants to the wounds, then replaced the bandages and tourniquets.

"How is he, Doc?" Sergeant Mays asked. "Is he going to make it?"

"Well, thanks to you guys, he has a chance," the medic responded. "You did well to stop the bleeding."

Ten minutes after the relief platoon got there, a helicopter marked with red crosses on the nose, sides, and underneath, landed in the open area right beside them. Two men jumped down from the U-H1 and, carrying a stretcher, ran to the wounded man

"Is he going to live?" Sergeant Mays asked as the Dust Off crew put Billy onto the stretcher.

"I can't promise anything, but he's got a chance," one of the Dust Off medics said. "We'll have him back at Third Field in less than half-an-hour."

"He had a basketball scholarship to Kentucky, did you know that?" Sergeant Mays asked. "He was going home next week and would have been playing for them next season."

"We've got to get him on board so we can get the drip going," one of the medics said.

"Thanks for coming after him."

"That's what we're paid to do. You men take care," the medic said as, with Billy on the stretcher now, they hurried back to the helicopter. The pilot looked out through his window and nodded at Sergeant Mays. Mays nodded back. The engine was still going and the rotor blades were spinning and popping overhead.

As soon as Billy was on board, the pilot pulled pitch and Sergeant Mays turned his back and covered his face against the debris as the helicopter lifted off, then lowered its nose and moved quickly forward, climbing as it gained transitional lift.

Brandywine was out in his depot yard inventorying transmissions when he heard the popping sound of cavitating rotor blades overhead. Looking up, he saw the Dust Off helicopter approaching Hotel Three.

Brandywine thought about the wounded soldier on board, knowing that if his wound required a Dust Off medevac, it had to be serious. It reminded Brandywine that even though he was now in a rather cushiony and safe position, the war was still going on, and men were still being killed and grievously wounded.

He felt a twinge of guilt.

Jane Grey was having a cup of coffee in the nurse's break room when she got the word to report immediately to surgery. Now, masked and gowned, she watched as Doctor Largent worked on the mangled left arm and leg of the young soldier on the operating table.

"Hemostat," Largent said, holding his rubber-gloved hand out. Jane put the instrument in his hand, and Largent used it to clamp onto a piece of shrapnel and pull it from the wound. "How is his blood pressure?"

"Holding," one of the other nurses said.

"Damn," Largent said, "I'm not going to be able to save the knee."

Jane looked at the leg, or what was left of it. The lower part of the leg, like the lower part of his arm, had been traumatically amputated. There was no question on the arm; the trauma was far enough down that they had been able to save the elbow. Taking care of it had been merely a matter of tying off the veins and closing a skin flap over the wound.

But the leg had been severed much higher up, and though Jane had some hope that they would be able to save his knee, she knew the chances were slim. Saving the knee was important because rehabilitation would be much easier for the young man if he was able to keep his knee.

But the damage was too severe. Jane could feel a collective let-down in the operating room when Doctor Largent's words confirmed what they already knew.

Largent lifted a hand to his forehead and left a

bloody smudge there. Quickly, Jane dampened a cloth in a sterile solution and wiped the blood away for him.

"Okay," Largent said. He pointed to a spot just above the knee. "We'll cut here."

When the operation was over, Jane went into the scrub room, peeled off her rubber gloves, then removed her mask and cap and walked over to the lavatory. She put her hands on the side of the sink and leaned there for a moment. Then she looked into the mirror. What she saw shocked her. The eyes that burned into her soul, she had seen before. She had seen them in the faces of the wounded and in the faces of the young soldiers who came to the hospital to visit their friends. She had seen it in the faces of the pilots in the Red Bull. And now she was seeing "the thousand yard stare," in her own eyes.

"Who are you?" she asked her mirror image. "I don't even know who you are, anymore."

Jane washed her hands and splashed water onto her face. She held her hands over her face for a long moment.

"I won't cry," she said. "I won't cry."

She wondered how old the young soldier was. He couldn't have been over nineteen, maybe no older than eighteen.

Last year, at this time, the same boy was no doubt haunting the local high school hang out. She imagined him in a blue and white letter jacket, drinking a milkshake, listening to the juke box and:

"Watching some girl shake it," she said aloud.

"I beg your pardon?"

Startled, Jane looked around and saw that Doctor Largent had come into the room. The front of Doctor Largent's gown was soiled with blood.

"I, uh, asked if you think he is going to make it?"

"Depends on what you mean by make it," he answered. "He will live. But without an arm and a leg, he's going to have a rough time of it."

"These are the ones who will haunt my memory for the rest of my life," Jane said. "I mean, we have them die in here every day, and we get a body count every week. For the ones who are killed, it's all over. But for that young soldier in there," she paused. "Fifty or sixty years from now he will look at the empty space in his shirt and pants, and he'll be nineteen again, reliving the hell of this war."

She spun away from him and began splashing water on her face again.

"Are you going to be okay?" Largent asked.

Jane nodded, but said nothing.

"Jane, you knew, coming over here, that you were going to be exposed to things like this, didn't you?"

"Yes, but that doesn't make it any easier."

"No, it doesn't. And I pray that it never gets any easier for any of us, because if it did, I'm afraid we would lose our humanity, if not our souls."

"You're a good man, Doctor Largent."

Largent chuckled. "Do you mean that, or, are you just saying that because I authorized your trip to Vung Tau last month?"

"Oh, well, I confess that I was grateful to you for that. It was very . . . nice."

"I'm glad you enjoyed it. And I must say that everyone really kept the secret well. I mean, who would have thought that President Nixon could come over here and go back without anyone ever even hearing about it?"

"Doctor Largent, maybe I should tell you . . ."

Largent's laugh interrupted her. "You don't have to tell me anything," he said. "It didn't take me long to figure out that I had been had. I asked around about this guy, Brandywine. If I was had, from what I understand, I was had by one of the best."

"He is a . . . unique . . . person," Jane said. "Oh," she put her hand to your lips. "Doctor, you aren't going to . . . uh . . . do anything or you? I mean, like press charges or something?"

"Lord no," Doctor Largent said. "When you find someone like that, you don't make an enemy of him. You make friends. That way if you ever need something done, you know where to go to get it done."

"W can be a very good friend," Jane agreed.

The rainy season was in full force, and Brandywine stood on the balcony just outside a 7th floor room of the Continental Hotel, watching the rain move off the Saigon River and slash across the roofs of the city. In the alley alongside the hotel, two children sought shelter beneath a piece of corrugated tin, which they held over them. A bicyclist on Le Loi Avenue pedaled furiously through the rain, flipped over on the slick road, and slid into a stack of two-gallon tin containers that were being displayed by a sidewalk shopkeeper. The bicyclist limped off with bleeding legs and a damaged bike, followed by the curses of outrage from the peddler.

The rain was also falling on Brandywine, and his uniform hung heavy with water, but he made no attempt to escape. He loved the rain. It blanketed all sight and sound and formed a curtain behind which his soul could exist in absolute solitude. Only those with whom he really wanted to share could penetrate it.

From the time he realized that his marriage with Glenda was failing, Brandywine had been closing off his inner-self to others. He knew the marriage was failing midway through his first Vietnam tour. She came to Honolulu to meet him for R and R, but she treated him more like a fellow vacationer than a husband from whom she had been separated for several months.

It had not been Brandywine's intention to ever let anyone else in . . . until he met Jane Grey. She was pretty, bright, had a good sense of humor. That was very important to Brandywine, and fun to be with. He had meant her to be no more than a pleasant diversion, somebody to help him get through this last six months.

But he hadn't figured on being needed. Jane was facing her own trauma as, day after day, she saw bleeding and broken bodies. She also held the hands of young men for whom she was their last human contact, not their wives, not their mothers, but she.

Every night they had dinner and drinks at the club. They would later sit in the dark on the embankment just outside the hospital and watch movies, while in the distance the horizon flashed and the guns roared. And there came a time when holding hands and the occasional kiss in the dark weren't enough. It was actually Jane who suggested that they rent a room in the Continental Hotel, a majestic old hotel right in the heart of Saigon.

"W? You are standing in the rain?"

"Yeah," Brandywine replied, sheepishly. "It's kind of stupid, I guess, but I like the rain and . . ."

"No!" Jane interrupted. "Don't spoil it with an explanation. It would totally change everything I know about you if you tried to explain." She came out onto the balcony to stand with him.

"You'll get wet," Brandywine warned.

"It won't be the first time." She leaned into him, and he put his arm around her. "W, when you were a kid, did you ever dream about coming to exotic places?"

"I didn't have to dream about it. I went to Cairo, Illinois; that's about as exotic as it gets," Brandywine said. "What about you?"

Jane chuckled. "My dad owns a car dealership in

Dallas. The word exotic isn't even in the Texas language."

"Is there anyone back in Dallas waiting for you?" Brandywine asked. "Husband, boyfriend, pet gerbil?"

"I was engaged to a doctor," Jane said. "But when I refused to let him get me a deferment, he broke it off."

"I'm sorry."

"How are you handling your divorce?"

"I'm okay with it," Brandywine said. "I would have stuck it out . . . tried to salvage it. But I don't think that was possible, and to be honest, I guess I admire Glenda for having the courage to drop the hammer."

"You don't hate her?"

"Hate her? No, of course not. She is a part of my life, and there were some good times. You know, the Indians have a saying or maybe it's the Chinese or the Visigoths. I don't know exactly who," he said. "They say that the flower that blooms for a day does not differ at heart from the tree that lives for a thousand years."

Jane chuckled quietly. "It was the Visigoths, I'm sure."

"What it means is . . ."

"I know what it means, W," Jane said, interrupting him. "It means that every moment is important. This moment." She raised her lips to him and they kissed.

Jane shivered.

"Are you cold? You want to go inside and get a towel?" Brandywine asked.

"Might not be a bad idea," Jane said. "I hope you brought a change of uniform."

"Yeah, in my AWOL bag. You?"

"Yes."

They went inside and took off their shirts. Both were wearing OD tee shirts beneath the fatigue blouse. Jane's tee shirt was wet, and it made her nipples quite prominent.

"Never thought an Army tee-shirt could look so good," Brandywine said with a chuckle as he started to close the door.

"No," Jane said. "Leave it open."

"Okay, if that's what you want."

Outside, the rain continued to fall. The cocoon that Brandywine had built around himself became tighter, and the idea of being inside that cocoon with Jane was a sensual one.

"I brought a bottle of wine," Brandywine said.

"A glass of wine would be nice," Jane agreed.

Brandywine reached down into his AWOL bag and took out a bottle. "I would give you a choice of red or white, but I only have red."

"In that case, I'll take red. Did you bring glasses?"

"Sort of."

"Sort of?"

"In the AWOL bag. You can have the pretty one."

Jane retrieved the glasses, one a clean peanut butter jar, with the Skippy label still intact, the other a decorated jelly glass.

"Jane?"

She looked over at him.

"I like this," Brandywine said as he began working the cork from the bottle.

Taking the wine over to the sofa, Brandywine filled the two jars. Jane sat, taking off her boots and socks, and then pulled her legs up under her. She took a sip, and capturing a beam of light from the lamp on the end table, the burgundy gave off a burst of color.

"So, what have you been doing all day, besides standing out in the rain?" Jane asked, smiling brightly.

"I flew some pitch-change links up to Phu Loi," he said. "Whoop de do."

"Do you miss doing the recovery flights?"

"Yeah. I never thought I would hear myself say this, but I guess I do."

"Why?"

"Did you ever see the movie, *Mr. Roberts*? Do you remember the roll Henry Fonda played? How he felt burned out by sailing from tedium to boredom day in and day out? That's me."

"Yes, but the difference is Mr. Roberts had not been in action, and you have."

"Yeah, I guess," Brandywine said. "But what about you? Tell me about your day."

"We had a traumatic amputee today, an arm and a leg," she said. "Young, nineteen maybe, twenty at the most." She shook her head. "That's really all I want to say about it."

"All right," Brandywine said, not pressing her any further.

Brandywine put his glass down and moved closer to her. He leaned toward her, and she came to him with her lips already parted.

Brandywine felt the hot satin of her tongue darting into his mouth, seeking his. The kiss was hot and slow and long, and it grew until it began to take control of each of them. Almost as if of its own volition, Brandywine's hand dropped to her hip. Even through the material of her damp fatigue trousers, he could feel the heat of her body, and he knew that her trembling was half from fear and half in excitement.

At last they came up for breath and when she looked at him, her eyes were deep and diaphanous, and he could see all the way to the bottom . . . to the Jane inside. The Jane inside was not the self-assured, Army lieutenant, combat nurse. The Jane inside was elementary, hopeful, and very vulnerable.

At that moment Brandywine was both possessive and protective, primeval man, unsure as to whether to defend her or ravage her.

"W?" she said. Her voice sounded small and far away. "Whether we go any further with this or stop now . . . it is entirely up to you. I only ask that you do not leave a scar on my soul."

Brandywine led her to the bed. Once again, he started to close the door.

"No," Jane protested. "Leave it open, please. I like to hear the rain."

"All right," Brandywine agreed. They were standing little more than a breath apart, and he saw her as if looking through gauze, in a room that was gray with late afternoon rain light.

Jane turned her back and pulled the tee shirt over her head. Then she gave him a silent invitation to undo her bra. Barely in control of his shaking hand, he undid the bra, then watched her slip out of it. With her back still to him, Jane stepped out of her trousers and wearing only panties lay the trousers on the chair by the bed. Brandywine turned back the covers and, smiling nervously, Jane slid into bed, exposing herself just for the space of a heartbeat.

From beneath the sheet, Jane raised her hips and then her legs. Her hand came out from under the covers with the ounce or so of lace and silk that she dropped to the floor. Brandywine was so mesmerized by it all that he had made no effort to begin undressing.

"Are you having second thoughts?" Jane asked.

"What? No," Brandywine answered, surprised by the question. "Why would you think that?"

Jane smiled. "Because, W, my dear, you are there, fully dressed, and I am here, totally naked."

"Oh," Brandywine said. Quickly, he pulled his shirt over his head, then, sitting on the edge of the bed, slipped out of his boots, trousers, and underwear. Nude, he slid under the sheet.

Jane turned to him, and as her body molded against his, his heart began to hammer. He breathed the scent of her with his kiss. His hand trailed across her smooth skin and she moaned in pleasure as her own hands began to explore his body. They kissed again, a kiss that went beyond passion to become one of exploration and wonder. It was a lover's kiss that was unique in all the world, because it had a taste that was neither hers nor his, but theirs.

When the time was right, Brandywine moved over her. He knew, intuitively, not to rush. He gave her what she desired and needed, but more than that, he gave her what she wanted, but dared not ask for.

Through the open door, which led onto the balcony, they could hear the rain. It was like perfectly orchestrated music, with rhythmic percussion: harmonic bass notes from the larger drops and delicate trills and melodious tinkling from the water that dripped off the eaves and cascaded onto the balcony floor. Occasionally a little spray of mist would drift into the room to land upon their skin, skin that was so hot that Brandywine was surprised when he didn't hear it sizzle.

As they continued to make love all thought and awareness of anything beyond themselves ceased.

There was only pleasure, the feel of her tongue against his, the rake of her fingernails across his back, and the soft, suppleness of her body, molded so completely against him.

A helicopter passed overhead, and for one brief moment Brandywine felt as if he were in both places at once— here in bed with this vulnerable woman and up there in the red glow of the instruments and the winking lights of the city below.

A drenched pigeon, seeking shelter from the rain, landed under the eaves of the balcony and fluttered its feathers, but they were unaware of its presence.

Chapter Nineteen

Brandywine grabbed the telephone on the first ring. "Open storage, Mister Brandywine."

"Sniff snert snarc."

"Hello, Captain Fender, what can I do for you?"

"Award ceremony today, seventeen hundred. Sniff."

"Seventeen hundred? Okay, I'll be there."

"Have you seen Colonel Cleaver yet?"

"No, not yet."

"Not yet?"

"It's not my fault. I've been there several times, but for some reason the colonel hasn't been able to fit me into his schedule yet. I'll keep trying though."

"Sniff, snert, snarc, honk, snort?"

"Yes, I promise. I will keep trying."

"Sniff," Captain Fender said as he hung up the phone.

It was about five minutes after five by the time Brandywine made it over to the 65th. When he got there, the company was already in parade formation, with First Sergeant Muldoon standing out front and all the platoon sergeants in their respective positions. Because the first sergeant was, for the moment, in charge of the company, and an NCO cannot be in charge of officers, the platoon leaders were not in formation but were standing behind their respective platoons.

Major Casey, Captain Fender, Lieutenant Kirby, and B. Dowling Mudd were waiting just outside the door to the orderly room. Kirby was wearing khakis.

Captain Fender was wearing jodhpurs, highly polished knee-boots, an ivory-handled pistol, and he was carrying a riding quirt.

Captain Hicks, who was standing behind the formation waiting to post, had on a MacArthur style hat, oversized sun-glasses, a corn-cob pipe, a long, white-silk scarf, and a sweeping, handlebar moustache.

Colonel Cleaver stepped out of the orderly room. Brandywine had been back in country for three months now, nearly half of his extension, and had successfully avoided seeing Cleaver all that time. He had no desire to run into him now, so he stayed back in the vicinity of the bulletin board to lessen the likelihood of his being seen.

"Company!" First Sergeant Muldoon shouted.

"Platoon!" the word rippled up and down the formation as the platoon sergeants replied with the supplemental commands.

"A-tenn-shunn!"

Brandywine was not a part of the formation, so he didn't come to attention. Instead, he folded his arms across his chest and leaned back against the bulletin board to watch the proceedings.

Major Casey stepped to the front of the formation. He turned to take Muldoon's report.

"Sir, Sixty-fifth Transportation Company all present and accounted for," Muldoon said, saluting sharply.

Casey returned his salute and then called "Post!"

The platoon leaders now moved forward. Before going home on leave, Brandywine had been acting platoon leader of headquarters platoon, and curious to see who would have the platoon now he leaned forward to take a look. There, standing at attention in front of the platoon, proudly wearing his lavender Nehru jacket, gaudily decorated with several layers of gold chain, was Unsoldier.

"I'll be damned," Brandywine said, with a quiet chuckle.

"Lieutenant Jefferson Freemont Kirby, front and center!" Major Casey called.

Kirby presented himself at the front and center of the formation. At the same time, Kirby came up and

Colonel Cleaver also came over from where he had been standing.

Captain Fender began to read aloud.

"Sniff, sniff, snert! Attention to orders!" He looked out over the company to make certain that everyone was actually paying attention to orders.

"On thirteen February while engaged in a combat recovery operation near Dak Tho, RVN, First Lieutenant Jefferson Freemont Kirby distinguished himself under fire.

"Despite withering, aimed, automatic weapon's fire, from which Lieutenant Kirby sustained a wound, he, at great personal risk, single-handedly engaged with and captured an enemy sniper whose deadly accurate fire could have put the entire mission in jeopardy.

"For his intrepidity, bold leadership, and mission performance above and beyond the call of duty, First Lieutenant Jefferson Freemont Kirby is hereby awarded the Bronze Star with "V" device."

After reading the entire document without sniffing once, Captain Fender stuck his inhaler into his nose for several desperate sniffs.

Kirby saluted Colonel Cleaver, who pinned the Bronze Star to the front of his shirt.

"Attention to orders," Fender said again. "Sniff, sniff, snert."

"For wounds sustained in action on thirteen February, while engaged in a combat recovery operation near Dak Tho, RVN, First Lieutenant

Jefferson Freemont Kirby is hereby awarded the Order of the Purple Heart."

Again, Kirby saluted and stepped forward as, this time, Major Casey pinned the Purple Heart to the front of his shirt.

"First Sergeant!" Major Casey called, and once more, the first sergeant came forward to take charge of the company. With that, all the platoon officers left and started toward the Wet Mouse.

Brandywine started to leave as well, but Major Casey called over to him.

"Mister Brandywine, come on into the lounge!" he called. "The sun is over the yardarm . . . we'll wet down Kirby's medals."

Miss Song, who had been Brandywine's secretary back when he was the property book officer, doubled as the Wet Mouse bartender. She handed Brandywine a beer as soon as he came in.

"Thanks, Miss Song," Brandywine said. He lifted his beer to his lips and looked over at Lieutenant Kirby.

"How does that citation read now, Lieutenant?" Brandywine asked. "Something about intense aimed *enemy* fire? Oh, yes, and something about you single handedly capturing a VC prisoner?" Brandywine put his hands in the air. "*Chieu Hoi*," he said, laughing quietly. *Chieu Hoi.*"

"Are you . . . are you going to make something out of it?" Kirby asked.

"Me . . . make trouble?" Brandywine replied. He shook his head. "Not me, Kirby. I'm a real, easy-going guy."

"Mister Brandywine, I want to congratulate you for the way you have been running the open depot," Major Casey said. "It used to be that only the screw ups got there. Now I've got people standing in line wanting to go there."

"They just like the Saturday morning champagne breakfasts," Brandywine said.

Casey chuckled. "Yes, I believe I did hear something about that. And you are letting them wear red baseball caps, I understand."

"Just something to help with the esprit de corps," Brandywine said.

"Well, you are doing a fine job. But then you always have. That's why you get away with all the shit you pull."

"I try, sir," Brandywine answered.

"I see you managed to get rid of Mr. Capp."

"Yes, sir."

Cleaver had stepped into the officers' latrine as soon as he went into the Wet Mouse and now, as he came out, he saw Brandywine for the first time. For a long moment, he just stared at Brandywine, and Brandywine returned his gaze as he waited for the axe to fall.

"Mister Brandywine," Colonel Cleaver said, speaking in the low, clipped tones that suggested he was a man who was trying desperately not to lose his temper. "Do you know your rights under Article Thirty-two?"

"Am I being charged with something, Colonel?"

"Do you know your rights under Article Thirty-two?" Colonel Cleaver repeated, a little louder this time.

"Yes, sir, I know my rights."

"You are authorized counsel before I start questioning you about your status as a deserter."

"Deserter?" Major Casey said. "Colonel Cleaver, what are you talking about, deserter?"

"All right, AWOL, then."

"No, sir," Brandywine said. "I returned on time, in accordance with the requirements of my leave. In fact, you can check the company book and see when I signed in."

"That's true, Colonel," Casey said. "He got back here the day he was supposed to. Where did you get the idea he was AWOL?"

"All right, all right, failure to repair then," Colonel Cleaver said with an impatient wave of his hand. He pointed at Brandywine. "Maybe you got back in country when you were supposed to, but you were supposed to report to battalion headquarters on the first day you got back. You did not report on that day, so I intend to court-martial you."

"Colonel, I beg your pardon, sir, but I did report to battalion headquarters on that day," Brandywine said.

"What?" Cleaver replied angrily, slamming his fist down so hard on the bar that it knocked Captain

Hick's beer over, spilling it onto Fender's jodhpurs. "Mister, are you going to stand right here in front of me and tell me a bold-faced lie? Do you think I don't know whether or not you reported to battalion headquarters? You have not!"

"Yes, sir, I have," Brandywine said. "And if you will check your sign-in roster at your headquarters, you will see that I have reported in every morning for the last ninety days, at exactly o-nine-hundred hours. The problem is your staff would not let me in to see you because I didn't have an appointment."

"What do you mean . . . you didn't have an appointment?" Cleaver said, so angry now that his face had turned red and his temple was throbbing.

"You do require an appointment for people to see you, do you not, sir?" Brandywine asked.

"Yes, of course I do," Cleaver replied. "Otherwise I would not be able to arrange my day."

"Yes, sir, and I find that a very commendable trait," Brandywine said. "You never made an appointment to see me."

"I never made an appointment to see you? Mister, since when, in this man's Army, does a colonel make an appointment to see a warrant officer?"

"Whenever I'm to report at your convenience, Colonel, and not my own," Brandywine replied. "You are commanding the three sixty-fifth Aviation Battalion. That is a very responsible job, sir. In fact, I read that because of the unique nature of this war that battalion commanders have the most difficult job in Vietnam. It would seem to me that my imposing on you at this critical time would be the height of insubordination. Therefore, I chose to report every day at o-nine-hundred until you found the time in your busy schedule to see me."

"And what had you planned to do in the meantime? Just sit on your ass?"

"Oh, no sir," Brandywine replied. "I've been assigned as Officer in Charge of the Sixty-fifth Aviation Depot Open Storage."

"You what? What do you mean you have been assigned as OIC of Open Storage? I made no such assignment." Colonel Cleaver looked at Major Casey. "Did you assign him to open storage?"

"No sir, his orders are signed by Colonel Van Buren from Thirty-fourth Group," Major Casey said.

"You have orders directly from Thirty-fourth Group?" Colonel Cleaver looked at Brandywine. "You went over my head?"

"No sir, I have not spoken to Colonel Van Buren. I just assumed that, since you were too busy to see me directly, you had arranged this assignment."

"You, you . . . I . . . I . . ." Colonel Cleaver stuttered, so angry that he could barely speak. He turned to Captain Fender.

"Captain Fender!"

"Snit?" Fender replied, fearfully. He was still trying to brush the beer off his trousers.

"What the hell? What have you done to your inhaler?"

Fender's inhaler was decorated with the USARV patch.

"What inhaler, sir? Sniff?"

"Never mind," Colonel Cleaver said with a dismissive wave of his hand. He pointed toward Brandywine. "I order you to look into this. I want to find out if Mister Brandywine actually did sign in every morning. And I want to find out if he went down to Thirty-fourth Group to plead his case."

"Snarck, sir," Fender said.

Cleaver looked at his watch and then back toward the others. "I have a dinner engagement tonight with General Carney," he said. "Lieutenant Kirby, it is a pleasure to have a real hero in our midst. You gentlemen, carry on."

The officers came to attention and Casey saluted for them all. After Cleaver left, Casey turned to Brandywine.

"I hope you didn't personally go down to Thirty-fourth Group and lobby for your assignment," Casey said. "If you went over Cleaver's head, he's going to have your ass."

"I didn't . . . personally . . . go over his head," Brandywine said. He pulled several strips of chewing gum tinfoil from his pocket and handed them to Casey.

"Thanks," Casey said.

Shortly after Cleaver left several other officers came into the lounge, including some officers from some of the other companies within the battalion. Soon the lounge was full with at least twenty-five or thirty officers, and they were gathered in so many conversational groups that the noise level inside the club was an incomprehensible babble.

Brandywine saw B. Dowling Mudd sitting alone at a table in the far corner of the room, and he moved over to join him.

"You talked your way out of another one," B. Dowling Mudd said.

"So it would appear," Brandywine said, taking a swallow of his beer. "So it would appear."

"Is Captain Fender going to find anything on you?"

"Nope."

"Are you saying there is nothing to find?"

"I'm saying he isn't going to find anything on me."

"One of these days, Brandywine, you are going to get yourself into more trouble than you can get out of."

"No way."

"What makes you so certain that's not going to happen?"

Brandywine feinted a punch toward B. Dowling Mudd, then jerked it back. "Because I'm like Muhammad Ali," he said. "I float like a butterfly; I sting like a bee."

"Yes, well, Cassius Clay stepped on his root with the U.S. Government. You haven't seen him in the ring lately, have you?" B. Dowling Mudd asked. "And you are going to wind up doing the same thing."

"As it turns out, I'm not the only one working the system," Brandywine said as he took a swallow of his beer.

"What do you mean?"

"Your boy Kirby just picked up a couple of medals he didn't earn."

"No, you're wrong. He really did capture an enemy soldier," B. Dowling Mudd said.

"I made that mission with him, remember?"

B. Dowling Mudd stroked his chin for a moment. "That's right you did, now that I think about it. That was the one where Ray went down, wasn't it?"

"Yes."

"Well, what happened? I mean, Kirby did come back with a prisoner and a wound."

"The prisoner was a *chieu hoi*, and the wound came from a thorn prick. The machine gun fire came from the rounds cooking off in the ammo chutes of Ray's ship."

"You mean he has just been awarded medals that he didn't earn?"

"That's what I mean."

"But that's not right. If he didn't earn those medals then somebody should do something. The Army should take them back," B. Dowling Mudd said.

"How is that going to happen?"

"Well, I don't know. If nothing else, I'll go tell the Army what really happened."

"Tell them whatever you want," Brandywine said. "His medals are a part of official Army records now."

"How did that information get into the official records?"

"It came from Kirby's after action report," Brandywine said.

"But his after action report is a lie."

"Why, B. Dowling Mudd, what are you saying?" Brandywine asked, affecting a shocked look. "Are you suggesting that an officer would lie on his after-action report . . . just to make himself look good?"

"You were there, Brandywine," B. Dowling Mudd said. "You could tell the Army what really happened."

"Why should I?"

"Because it isn't right," B. Dowling Mudd said again. "And you know it isn't right."

"Yeah, I know," Brandywine said. He smiled and took another swallow of his beer. "And what's better, he knows that I know. No. I think I'll just let the son of a bitch sweat."

As the evening wore on, Kirby, worrying about whether or not Brandywine was going to tell what really happened, began to drink quite heavily. Soon he was obviously drunk, and Brandywine moved around behind the bar.

"Do you want another beer?" he asked Kirby.

"What . . . what are you going to do?" Kirby asked. Kirby was having a hard time focusing.

"I'm going to give you another beer," Brandywine said, taking a beer from the refrigerator. "And I'll even pay for it."

There was a piece of paper on the refrigerator door with everyone's name listed. As each person got a beer, they would put a mark by their name and would settle up at the end of the month. Brandywine put the mark by his name.

"Why are you doing this?" Kirby asked. "Why are you being so nice to me? I don't trust you."

"Well, don't forget. I was out there with you when the bullets started flying," Brandywine said. "And I saw the way you handled that prisoner. Here, let me open this for you."

"I can open," Miss Song said, reaching for the beer.

"No, no, no, that's all right," Brandywine said, waving her off. "I'll do it. Lieutenant Kirby is a genuine war hero, don't you know? It would be an honor for me to punch holes in his beer can."

Brandywine picked up the beer-can opener that was hanging from the bar by a leather boot string. He punched a hole in the top of the can, turned it not one hundred eighty degrees, but forty-five degrees, where he punched a second hole.

"Mister Blandeewine?" Miss Song started, but Brandywine held his finger to his lips.

"Shh," he said. He handed the beer to Kirby. "Here you go, my good man," he said. "Drink it down."

A few others at the bar had noticed the way Brandywine punched the holes in the can, and they watched in fascination as Kirby turned the beer up to his lips. As he did so, a solid, golden stream of beer poured down from the hole on the side, getting the front of his shirt wet.

"I know some people might not under . . ." Kirby started. He then noticed the beer pouring out on him. He turned the can to the other hole.

"I know some people might . . ." he started again, but once more the beer poured out on his shirt. Shrugging, he continued to drink. "Not understand me, but I must keep myself politically viable. And a good military record will do that. Look at John Kennedy."

"John Kennedy? Are you comparing yourself to President Kennedy?"

"Why not? Have you ever noticed our initials? JFK." Kirby wagged his finger back and forth. "I don't believe that is by mere chance. I think it is fate."

"Fate, huh?" Brandywine said.

"Fate," Kirby said again, his head falling onto the bar.

Brandywine picked it up and then let it drop again.

"Damn, what happened to our hero?" Captain Hicks asked as he twirled his long, handlebar moustache. "Did he pass out?"

"It would appear so," Brandywine said. Coming from behind the bar, he turned the stool around and let Kirby fall across his shoulder as he picked him up. "I'm leaving anyway; I'll put him to bed."

"Well, Mister Brandywine, that is certainly very nice of you," Major Casey said.

"Well, you know me, Major Casey. I am a very nice kind of a guy. Right, B. Dowling Mudd?"

B. Dowling Mudd just stared with disapproval as Brandywine, with Kirby tossed over his shoulder, started toward the door.

Brandywine left, but for the rest of the evening, as the beer flowed and the bladders filled, those who were celebrating Kirby's medals would step into the officers' latrine to relieve themselves. They had to be very careful where they went, though, because the subject of their celebration, the hero of the hour, First Lieutenant Jefferson Freemont Kirby, was lying in one end of the urinal, an arm and leg hanging over the edge.

Chapter Twenty

Captain Fender stood in front of Specialist Clark's desk, waiting, as Clark checked the appointment book. Fender was wearing a Civil War era dress-blue uniform, complete with a gold-lined cape. A gilt-handled sword in a chrome scabbard was thrust through a gold cummerbund.

"And, what was your name again, sir?" Clark asked.

"Fender. Captain Fender."

"Are you in our Army, Captain Fender?"

"Snert? Snit, sniff, snarck!" Fender sniffed angrily.

"Ahh, here it is, sir. Yes, sir, you do have an appointment. You can go right in."

"Snock."

"You're welcome, sir."

Captain Fender went into Colonel Cleaver's office carrying the visitor's sign-in book, as well as an extract of the set of orders from 34th Group headquarters, assigning Brandywine as Officer in Charge of the 65th Aviation Depot Open Storage.

"Snit," he said, putting the book down on Cleaver's desk. He started pointing out Brandywine's name, date, and time of sign-in. "Sniff, snert, snarck," he said each time his finger found the name.

"Are you sure?"

"Snock," Fender sniffed, nodding. "Every morning at o-nine-hundred, ever since he has been back. That's a total of seventy-one days, excluding Sundays and Saturdays."

"Clark!" Cleaver shouted, angrily. "Get in here!"

Specialist Clark hurried in to respond to Cleaver's call. "Yes, sir?"

"Is it true that Mister Brandywine has reported in here every morning at o-nine-hundred since," he looked at the book, "Six February?"

Clark nodded. "Oh, yes, sir, just as regular as clock work," he said.

"Why the hell didn't you send him in to see me?"

Clark got a confused and hurt look on his face. "Sir, didn't you tell me you would only see people who had an appointment?" Clark asked.

"Well, yes, but . . ."

"I assumed that meant officers as well as enlisted men. Yes, sir, now that I think about it, I know that included officers as well as EM. I have a copy of Battalion SOP if you would like to see it," Clark said.

"No, that's not necessary," Cleaver said with a frustrated sigh. He thumped the sign-in book. "You are sure these are all his signatures?"

"Yes, sir."

"Didn't you wonder why he showed up every day?"

"No, sir. He is the morale officer. I know that's just a collateral duty, but I figured that he was just being conscientious . . . showing up every day."

"Moral officer? Who is the morale officer?"

"Why, Mister Brandywine is the morale officer," Clark said.

"What are you talking about?"

"He has a desk right here in the office," Clark said, pointing toward the door. "Would you like to see it?"

Colonel Cleaver walked to the door and looked over at the desk. On front of the desk was a sign, reading:

W.W. Brandywine, CW-3, AVN

Morale Officer, 365th AVN BN

There was also a framed picture of an older couple, standing by a Jersey Cow a'la "American Gothic."

"That's a photo of his mom and dad," Clark said, pointing to the picture. "They are farmers back in Sikeston, Missouri. That's where he is from, originally, you know. That's in the bootheel of Missouri."

"I don't care where he is from or where that is!" Cleaver said in frustration. He ran his hand through his hair as he looked at Clark. "How do you know all that?"

"Well, he talks to us when he is here working. He's an awfully nice guy."

"When he is here . . . working? Here . . . in this headquarters?"

"Yes, sir."

"You have actually seen him working here."

"Yes sir. Lots of times. He's a real good hearts player. You need to watch him. He'll drop that queen of spades on you in a military minute," Clark said.

"Sergeant O'Leary!" Cleaver called.

"Yes, sir?" O'Leary answered, looking up from his desk.

Cleaver pointed to Brandywine's desk. "Have you ever seen Mr. Brandywine?"

"Yes, sir, I've seen him every day since you appointed him the morale officer," Sergeant O'Leary replied.

"Since I appointed him morale officer? Has everyone in here gone crazy?"

"Sir," Sergeant O'Leary said. He picked up a clipboard from his desk. "Here are the orders with your signature."

Cleaver shook his head and went back into his office. "Let me see the extract that assigned him to open storage," he said.

Captain Fender handed the orders to him.

"Did you check on these? Are they authentic?"

"Sniff."

"Damn," he said. "All right, the son of a bitch has won this round. "But you mark my words, Fender. He hasn't heard the end of this."

"Snit," Fender agreed.

When Brandywine came to the 365th Headquarters the next day, Colonel Cleaver was waiting for him. So was everyone else in the headquarters but not at their desks. Colonel Cleaver had everyone standing along one wall. None of the desks were in their normal position but had been pushed together in one long line.

"Good morning, Colonel," Brandywine said. He saw all the desks pushed together.

"Are we having a house-cleaning?"

"Which desk is yours?" Cleaver asked.

"I beg your pardon, sir?"

"I am told that you have a desk here, and that you have actually been showing up for duty."

"Yes, sir."

"Then you won't have any trouble picking out which desk is yours, will you?"

"Well, I . . ."

"I'm waiting, Mister Brandywine."

Brandywine went over to look at the line of gray metal desks. There were no nameplates on any of them, nor was there any visible paperwork.

Brandywine feared that he would have to take a wild guess, then, beneath one of the desks, he saw a pair of Ho Chi Minh sandals, with toes pointed out, mimicking the way he walked.

"It's this desk, Sir," he said.

"Hrrmph," Colonel Cleaver said. "All right. Get the desks put back where they belong, and get to work." Disgruntled, he returned to his office.

Quickly, the desks were put back in place and refurnished.

"Were the clogs your idea, Clark?" Brandywine asked.

"No, sir, that was Sergeant O'Leary's idea," Clark said. "He's the one who noticed how you walk. The picture of your parents was my idea."

"What picture of my parents?"

"This picture," Clark said, putting a framed photograph of an elderly man and woman on the desk.

"That's not my parents."

"No, sir, I wouldn't expect it to be. I cut it out of the last issue of my *Successful Farming*."

"My God, it has finally happened," Brandywine said.

"What's that, Sir?"

"The patients are running the insane asylum."

Chapter Twenty-One

"Chief, this is McKay," Sergeant McKay said when Brandywine answered the phone. "We've got a problem with the jeep."

"What sort of problem?"

"The motor sergeant won't give me a trip ticket. Something about a cracked windshield."

"Hell, there's no telling how long that crack has been there."

"That's what I told him," McKay said. "But he's not going to issue it."

"All right. I'll come down there and see what I can do."

Brandywine caught a ride down to the motor pool on a duce-and-a-half. Hopping down in front of the checkout line, he saw Sergeant McKay leaning back against the jeep, proudly wearing the red baseball cap that denoted he was part of the open storage team. His arms were folded across his chest.

"Okay, what's going on?"

"You see this crack?" McKay asked, pointing to a crack about half an inch long in the lower right hand part of the windshield. "Sergeant Haverkost says that deadlines the vehicle."

"Let's go see him," Brandywine suggested.

There were at least twenty vehicles in line, waiting for dispatch. Sergeant Haverkost had the hood up on a three-quarter ton, checking the hoses around the engine.

"Sergeant Haverkost," Brandywine said.

Haverkost rose up and seeing the expression on Brandywine's face, held up his hand in defense. "Don't blame me, Chief," he said. "Colonel Cleaver said find some reason to deadline your jeep. Now, I like you, but you are a warrant officer. He is a colonel."

"Cleaver told you to find a way to deadline my jeep?" Brandywine asked in surprise.

"Yes, sir."

"I'll be damn." Brandywine took off his hat and ran his hand over his head. "And you are telling me that a tiny crack in the windshield will deadline the vehicle?"

"Yes, sir."

"I remember that jeep when Captain Martin was driving it. That crack has been there ever since I've been here," Brandywine said. "Why haven't you ever deadlined it before?"

"General Deegle never asked me to do it, Colonel Boil never asked me to do it. Only Colonel Cleaver."

"Let me see the ops manual. I want to see where it says that a tiny crack will deadline it."

"I thought you might want to see it, so I left it open," Haverkost said.

Brandywine went into the shop and looked at the operations manual. Haverkost pointed out the paragraph.

Any crack in the windshield shall be reason to deadline the vehicle until such time as the windshield can be replaced.

"You have any windshields in stock?" Brandywine asked.

"No, sir. Your quarter-ton will have to go EDP until the replacement windshield."

"How long will that take?"

"Well, if the requisition says the equipment is deadlined for parts, we'll get faster action. Maybe a week, two at the most."

Brandywine looked back down at the manual and saw something that made him chuckle. He looked up at Haverkost.

"How long if it isn't EDP?"

"A long time," Haverkost said. "Why wouldn't you want it to go EDP?"

"Do you have goggles?"

"Goggles?"

"Yes, you know, goggles," Brandywine said, making circles with his thumbs and forefingers before placing them over his eyes.

"Yes, sir, I've got goggles. Two for every vehicle in the TO&E, just like the book says. Why do you ask that?"

"Because it says here that you don't even need a windshield if the driver and front seat passenger have goggles."

Looking around the shop, Brandywine saw a shovel. He picked it up and started toward his jeep. "Sergeant McKay, draw two pair of goggles and get the trip ticket."

"Here, Mister Brandywine, what are you going to do?" Haverkost asked.

To the shocked surprise of everyone waiting in line, Brandywine began smashing out the windshield.

McKay laughed out loud. "Try and stop *my* chief," he said.

As Brandywine started back toward the shop, he saw Colonel Cleaver's Ford LTD Sedan come into the motor pool. With the privilege of rank, the LTD moved to the front of the line, and the Specialist-4 who was driving it got out. Unlike the others, who were wearing fatigues, the colonel's driver was in short-sleeve khakis. He wore dark, horn-rimmed glasses, and his hair, while within the limits allowed by regulations, was noticeably longer than that of the other soldiers. Taking a cloth from the front seat, he rubbed out an imaginary spot on the shining hood of the car.

As Brandywine passed by the car, he happened to glance toward the windshield. Seeing a small crack, he leaned over to examine it closely.

"Sergeant Haverkost, do you see this crack?"

"Yes, sir," Sergeant Haverkost said.

"So, if the question comes up, you will verify that you did see this crack?"

"Yes, sir. Mister Brandywine, you don't expect me to deadline the colonel's car, do you?"

"No," Brandywine said. "I don't."

"No, Chief," McKay called out to him. "Chief, you better think about that."

"Are you the colonel's driver?" Brandywine asked the specialist.

"Yes, sir."

"You'd better draw a couple pair of goggles."

"I beg your pardon?"

"You need this car today?"

"Yes, sir, I'm driving the colonel up to Ben Hoa."

"You'd better check out some goggles," Brandywine said again.

Then, to the absolute shock of the driver, Brandywine smashed the shovel against the windshield of the car.

"Ahhhiieee!!!" the colonel's driver screamed in a high-pitched shout. He put his hands to his cheeks and looked on in horror as the smashed, safety-plate glass was pulled out.

"Brandywine, what the hell are you doing?"

Captain Hicks asked, coming up at that moment. His own jeep was fourth in line.

Captain Hicks was now wearing a flak jacket, with no shirt beneath it. He wasn't wearing a hat but had a camouflage band tied around his head. His face was streaked with green grease paint, and he had a Bowie knife strapped to one arm. He was carrying an M-16.

"Colonel Cleaver's orders. Any vehicle with a cracked windshield is to be deadlined," Brandywine explained. "But, if you take the windshield out, then it can be issued with two pair of goggles."

"Colonel Cleaver's orders?" Hicks asked.

"Tell him, Haverkost. Did he tell you to deadline my quarter-ton because of a crack in the windshield?"

"Well, not . . ."

"You mean he didn't tell you to deadline my vehicle? You did it on your own?"

"No, sir," Haverkost said. "He told me to."

"There's your answer, Captain Hicks," Brandywine said.

"You want help in taking out the windshields?" Captain Hicks asked.

"I could use help," Brandywine said. "So many windshields, so little time."

"Flamboyant, right?" Hicks asked, raising his M-16 and slamming home the bolt.

"Flamboyant," Brandywine replied.

"Out of the way!" Hicks shouted, waving at the waiting drivers. "Get out of the way." He put the M-

16 on automatic and blasted out the closest windshield.

"Holy shit!" one of the waiting drivers shouted. Leaping down from their vehicles the drivers ran for cover.

Hicks moved down the line, firing on full automatic. Windshields were popping out, empty cartridges were flying, the sound of automatic weapons fire filled the air until finally, standing at the end of the line of waiting vehicles, with smoke curling from the barrel of his rifle, Hicks thrust a clenched fist into the air.

"Son of a bitch! That was good!" he shouted. "That was some flamboyant!"

For a long moment, there was absolute silence. Then Brandywine heard McKay start the jeep behind him.

"Chief," he said. "Maybe we better get down to the depot."

Chapter Twenty-Two

First Lieutenant Jefferson Freemont Kirby got his second Purple Heart when a sniper took a pot shot at the recovery team, and he cut himself diving for cover under the crashed helicopter. The security team made quick work of the sniper, who had managed to get off only one shot. Kirby also got a "V" to his Air Medal for that same mission, having noted in his after-action report that he had landed in the face of "withering enemy fire."

Two days later, Kirby saw a Vietnamese hooch near the site of a recovery. The security platoon leader told him that the structure was abandoned and had been thoroughly checked out, but Kirby, unperturbed by the report, took it on his own to attack. Handing his Belle and Howell 8mm triple turret to PFC Hanlon, he put on his flack jacket, approached the little shack, and then turned to fix a John Wayne glare toward the movie camera. With a dramatic gesture that would have made the Duke proud, he pulled the pin on a grenade, deployed the spoon, held it for a few seconds, and then tossed it through the open door. He backed up against the side of the little hut.

There the film took an unplanned direction, when shrapnel from the grenade punched through the thin, mud-plaster wall.

This wound was more substantial than the other two had been, necessitating medical evacuation to the Philippines. Although the medic and field doctor who treated him denied yet another Purple Heart for what was a self-inflicted wound, he did manage to get one issued by the hospital personnel at Clark Field. This wound, which actually peppered his ass pretty good, got him an early drop from Vietnam. He had served a total of four months and four days.

On the very next morning after Kirby was evacuated, Captain Hicks and Captain Fender, dressed in long flowing, 17th century coats with cuffed sleeves, pantaloons decorated with ribbons, and cocked hats with long, swooping feathers, faced each other in the company street at dawn.

Each man was armed with a large caliber, smooth bore, cap and ball dueling pistol. Both men discharged their weapons. The ball from Fender's pistol smashed through the Plexiglas cover of the outside bulletin board. The ball from Hick's pistol punched through the back wall of the EM latrine. Hanlon was sitting on one of the holes, attending to his morning constitutional, when the ball tore through the Saigon Post he was reading.

The two officers were subdued before they could get their pistols recharged. They were then medically evacuated back to the States for what the shrink diagnosed as histrionic personality disorders.

The sudden loss of three pilots had the unexpected effect of returning Brandywine to his old job as recovery officer, sharing the duty with B. Dowling Mudd. It was in this capacity that he attended the pre-mission briefing. From the moment he arrived, Brandywine realized that this was not going to be a routine operation. That was obvious because the briefing officer was not Major Casey as it normally was, nor even Colonel Cleaver. The briefing officer was Colonel Clifton Van Buren from 34th Group Headquarters.

"Gentlemen," Colonel Van Buren said. "Two weeks ago President Nixon informed the nation that we would be launching attacks across the border into Cambodia. Our mission is a part of that operation known as *Toan Thang* or Total Victory.

"The primary objective for this incursion is to locate, attack, and destroy COSVN, which, as you may or may not know, is the Communists' Central Office for South Vietnam.

"Our attack today will take place at a point ten miles inside the Cambodian border near the village of Memot.

"That is the over-all picture. Each unit will have its own role to play and for your particular role, I now turn you over to Colonel Cleaver."

Cleaver took over the briefing then.

"Gentlemen," he said. "This is going to be a maximum effort. Our battalion has the assignment of inserting a company of ARVN infantry."

"ARVNS, not Americans?" someone asked.

"Army of the Republic of Vietnam . . . yes."

"Shit, I hate that," one of the pilots said. "The Vietnamese puke all over our helicopters."

The others laughed, but Cleaver held up his hand to signal for quiet.

"The ARVNS will be brought here by truck," he said. "They'll load on by o-nine-hundred. We pull pitch at o-nine-fifteen, and we'll coordinate our insertion with that of the other units so that we have maximum troops on the ground by ten fifteen. Any questions?"

"Colonel, we'll be near Parrot's Beak, right?"

"That's right."

"That place is like a hornet's nest. Anti-aircraft guns all over the place. And I'm not talking about AK-47s. I'm talking about flak. Air burst weapons."

"That's true. But we'll have Cobras and they'll fly cover."

"What about the Air Force?"

"What about the Air Force?" Cleaver repeated.

"Are they going to provide support?"

"I told you we'll have support from Cobras."

"That's well and good, Colonel, but you know that the Cobras do not have the stand-off capability the Air Force has."

"I have no intention of running to the Air Force every time we have a little problem," Colonel Cleaver said. "We will go in as a unit, depending upon our own resources. Is that clear?"

"Yes, sir."

"Recovery?"

"Yes, sir," B. Dowling Mudd replied.

"You will go into the LZ with the first insertion element."

"Excuse me, sir, but what do you mean by 'go in' with them?" B. Dowling Mudd asked.

"When they land, you land," Cleaver answered. "You will remain on the LZ until the last element has off-loaded its troops. When the last element leaves the landing zone, you will depart with them. Unless, of course, one of them is down. In that case, you will remain on the ground until all downed aircraft have been extracted."

"Colonel, excuse me," Brandywine said, "but are you out of your mind? From the first element until the last will be at least ten minutes. Are you saying we're to remain on the ground for ten minutes?"

"I realize that I am asking a lot of you," Cleaver said. "But you must understand that this situation is very critical. We cannot leave a downed helicopter in Cambodia. To do so would create an international incident of enormous consequences. We must get them all out, and the only way we can insure that is to have you on the ground until the last helicopter leaves."

"Hanlon, you stay behind this trip," Brandywine said as they were preparing the helicopter for the mission.

"Why is that, sir?" Hanlon asked, disappointed that he would not be going.

"If we are going to stay on the ground until the last element leaves, then I want to haul ass out of there as fast as we can. To do that, we'll need to keep the weight down," Brandywine explained. "Trapp, go through the rigging gear and take out anything that we don't absolutely have to have."

"Yes, sir," Trapp said.

B. Dowling Mudd had been checking the main rotor. He hopped down from the deck. "Everything looks good," he said.

"I've put Hanlon off, and I have Trapp lightening us up as much as he can," Brandywine said.

"Good idea."

"It won't make any difference."

"What do you mean . . . it won't make any difference?"

"The son of a bitch is trying to kill me, B. Dowling Mudd. He hates me, and he is trying to kill me."

B. Dowling Mudd chuckled. "Oh, I wouldn't say that. Besides, why are you taking it so personally? You aren't the only one on the helicopter, you know."

"I know," Brandywine said. "He's trying to kill us all."

B. Dowling Mudd was flying, and as the flight of thirteen helicopters beat their way northwest from Tan San Nhut, Brandywine sat with his hands folded, looking through the window at the helicopter nearest them. Because the formation was so tight, he could see into the closest helicopter quite easily, and he saw the South Vietnamese soldiers sitting on the bench seats, staring straight ahead, the fear in their faces evident, even from this distance.

By contrast, the face of the American, sitting in the door behind the M-60, couldn't be seen at all because it was covered by the dark faceplate of his flight helmet.

Playing over and over in his mind was the song, "San Francisco, Be Sure to Wear Some Flowers in Your Hair." In an effort to get the endless loop out of his head, Brandywine tried to think of other things and recalled the last few times he had been with Jane Grey.

They had managed a few more weekends together at the Continental Hotel as well as one more trip to Vung Tau. She had been a sanctuary for him, but he wasn't sure where this relationship was going nor even where he wanted it to go. Perhaps she really was a rebound from Glenda.

And even with Glenda, in the early days when they first met in Germany, it had been good. It wasn't until later that the marriage went bad. He had been burned once; he didn't want to be burned again.

"Paris Control, this is Hammer Flight Leader. ADIZ penetration at o-two-hundred Zulu."

The flight leader's radio-call interrupted Brandywine's musing.

"We're in Cambodia," B. Dowling Mudd said.

"Hammer Flight, this is lead. Begin descent now."

B. Dowling Mudd lowered the collective and they started down, the blades popping loudly as they cavitated through their own rotor wash.

Suddenly the world around them began exploding. Green tracer rounds, like beads on long strings, played among the descending helicopters. Airbursts from heavy anti-aircraft weapons filled the sky with flashes of orange and dirty puffs of brown and black.

Helicopters began going down, some under auto-rotation, some on fire, and some in pieces.

"Over there!" Brandywine shouted, pointing. "Trapp, get on 'im!"

Trapp's door gun opened up, firing at the gun position.

In less than two minutes, eight of the thirteen helicopters were down, leaving only four of the troop carriers, plus the recovery helicopter.

The four undamaged helicopters set down quickly, discharged their troops, and then took off. B. Dowling Mudd continued his approach.

"What the hell are you doing, B. Dowling Mudd? We can't sit down now!" Brandywine shouted.

"Our orders are to stay on the ground," B. Dowling Mudd said.

"Think about it," Brandywine said. "If we land now, we'll be shot to pieces, just like those poor shits who are down there. We've got to stay up until the gunships get here. We're the only air they've got."

Four of the downed helicopters were burning fiercely, one more was lying over on its side, and three appeared to be in one piece though the rotor blades were stopped. Tracer rounds were raking into survivors as they scrambled to get away from the carnage.

"You're right," B. Dowling Mudd said. "Okay, let's arrrgh . . ."

Several rounds burst through the aircraft, coming up through the chin bubble on B. Dowling Mudd's side. They also took some in the rotor blades, as evidenced by the sudden one-to-one vertical vibration, and the whistling of wind through the bullet holes.

Concurrent with B. Dowling Mudd's cry was a sudden lurch of the helicopter. Brandywine grabbed the controls and put the vehicle into a very tight turn. Another line of tracers headed toward them. There was a loud burst inside the cabin, and Brandywine felt his stomach rise to his throat as he thought they had taken an explosive round.

"We're hit, we're hit!" he shouted.

"No, no, it's the fire bottle!" Trapp yelled through the intercom. "It's okay. We took a round through the fire extinguisher."

"Dagen, Trapp, are either of you hit?" Brandywine called.

"No. We're all right," they answered. "How's Mister B. Dowling Mudd?"

"He's hit. I don't know how bad, and I don't have time to look. I'm going to call the gunships in. Put down as much fire as you can. And if you locate a VC position, drop smoke."

"Yes, sir."

"Gunslinger, this is Good Nature Three. Where the hell are you?"

"This is Gunslinger. We're right behind you," a disembodied voice said in Brandywine's headset.

"Chief, we've got three of 'em marked," Dagen said.

Brandywine made another tight turn, just inside a long string of tracer rounds.

"Gunslinger, you see smoke?"

"Roger green, yellow, red," Gunslinger said.

"Positions are just east of the smoke."

Almost as soon as he got the words out, Brandywine saw two rocket plumes streaking by, followed by two explosions in one of the NVN gun positions.

"We've got you covered, Goodnature Three. Now, get that truck the hell out of our way."

"Haulin' ass," Brandywine said.

Although he was not technically authorized to be there, both Jane and Major Largent arranged for Brandywine to wait in the scrub room. He had no idea how long he was there. It could have been fifteen minutes, and it could have been two hours. It was as if his brain had been put on hold.

When, finally, Jane came in from ER, he knew before she said a word.

"No," he said, his eyes filling with tears. "No, not B. Dowling Mudd."

"W," Jane said. "Oh, W, I'm so sorry. There was nothing we could do."

She came to him and held him, as Brandywine wept in real tears and racking sobs.

Chapter Twenty-Three

Brandywine had been back in Fort Eustis, Virginia, for just over a month, and was now Chief of the Aviation Maintenance Officers' Course. That part was fine. What he didn't like was the fact that two weeks after he assumed this duty, Emile Cleaver arrived as the new commandant of the U.S. Army Transportation School. To make matters worse, Cleaver was now a full colonel.

Brandywine had just picked up his mail and was sitting at his desk in his office reading a letter from Jane.

> *Dear W,*
>
> *I miss you. I really miss you, but it's not just me. Even Doctor Largent says it's not the same without you. No screaming Cleaver, no duels at dawn, no smashed windshields.*
>
> *Wait until I tell you what the latest buzz is. Unsoldier is gone. But before you start to*

*worry about him, let me say he has gone
conventional. A new company has moved in to
compete with RMK. The company is called
Halliburton, and they seem to be doing an all
right job under Unsoldier's watchful eye. He
could go far with that company, but who would
ever know because nobody really knows what
his name is.*

*Major Casey is back in the States. He
retired in Florida, I think. He asked McKay
to build a shipping crate to take his tinfoil ball
home with him. I would love to be a fly on the
wall when he tries to explain that thing to his
wife. It is now eight-feet wide, so it is oversized
for a shipping crate. Mack finally convinced
him to break it down into seven or eight
smaller pieces. It's awful to see a grown man
cry.*

*Do you remember Lieutenant Kirby? How
can I ask that? Of course you do. After all,
you had to carry him out of the jungle after his
first Purple Heart. That thorn prick could
have maimed him for life. Well, some of the
guys were watching Stateside news footage, and
they swear they saw him sitting behind Jane
Fonda at a peace rally. I think they are wrong.
He was a weird duck, but even he wouldn't
stoop to that level. But, maybe, "when you go
to San Francisco, wear some flowers in your
hair," got to him too. That song is like a siren,
calling us all.*

Sometimes, when I lay awake at night,

(sleep seems so foreign to me now) I see the frightened faces of the young, soul-scarred men who have passed through here. I think of B. Dowling Mudd, and Ray Lambdin, and Dan Morris, and so many others, and I wonder if it has all been worth it.

Brandywine, it just goes on and on. How will this all end? I have the feeling that, even if we all pulled out and went home tomorrow, this war has so scarred us all, that it will be with us until the last of us is dead.

We will all carry a little bit of shame, and a lot of pride. But those who weren't here will never understand.

I didn't mean for this to wind up so maudlin. But I said I missed you, and I don't have anyone who can make me laugh, and forget this living hell.

I do hope things are going well for you, W. Please take care of yourself.

Love, Your Lady Jane

"Mister Brandywine, can you cover the first hour of my class for me?" Sergeant Dawes asked. "I've got to pick up my car from the shop."

"Yeah, sure," Brandywine said. Folding his letter, Brandywine stepped into the classroom that was adjacent to his office and gave an hour-long lecture on the principles of hydraulics. It was an easy class, one he had given many times over the years, not only during this and a previous assignment at the transportation school, but also at the Army Aviation School in Fort Rucker, Alabama, going all the way back to when he was an enlisted instructor before going to flight school.

Brandywine was nearly finished with the class when suddenly, and unexpectedly, he produced a trumpet from beneath the podium. As always, the reaction from the class was one of surprise. He raised the trumpet to his lips and played the opening bars of "Tijuana Brass."

The students laughed, and a few applauded.

"Now," Brandywine said. He pointed to the valves. "What I just did was give you a practical demonstration as to how, by moving valves so as to align passages, you can change the direction of flow. In this case it was air, but next hour Sergeant Dawes will discuss hydraulic servos with you. When he starts talking about redirecting the hydraulic fluid, think of the valves in this trumpet, and you will understand the principles." He glanced up at the big clock on the back wall.

"It's time for a ten minute break."

After the break, three young officers, one a warrant officer-one, and two first lieutenants, came up to talk to him. All three were carrying copies of his book, which they held out for him to sign.

"Put in there that you were my instructor, and I was the best student you ever had," one of the lieutenants said.

"I'll do it," Brandywine said with a chuckle. "But when they see all the lies I told in the book, do you really think they will believe this?" He put in the comment and signed his name.

"Mister Brandywine?" Sergeant Dawes said, coming into the classroom then. "Colonel Cleaver is on the phone."

"Thanks, Sarge," Brandywine said. Quickly, he signed the other two books as well and stepped from the classroom into the office.

"This is Mister Brandywine, sir," he said.

"Brandywine, meet me in General Redling's office in half an hour," Colonel Cleaver said.

Brandywine had no idea what this was all about, but when he showed up at the General's office, he saw a photographer from the PIO. Smiling, the General stepped up to him and handed him a sheet of paper.

"This is for you," General Redling said.

Brandywine examined it.

HEADQUARTERS
USARV
APO U.S. FORCES 96307
SPECIAL ORDER NUMBER 291   28 APR 1970
EXTRACT

14. DA 348. By direction of the Secretary of the Army, following individual is awarded the
DISTINGUISHED FLYING CROSS.

BRANDYWINE, WALTER WINCHELL, W2123490
ADMINISTRATIVE DATA
Auth: Para 3-58, Sec XV LTR 15 APR 1970
HOR: Sikeston, Missouri
PLEAD: Fort Rucker, Alabama
Award will be presented by CG of Ft. Eustis, VA

                              FOR THE COMMANDER
                              T.J. HUNSINGER

Colonel, GS
Chief of Staff
OFFICIAL:
ROBERT A. BIVENS
1LT, AGC
Asst Adj Gen
DISTRIBUTION: 110 AG Gen Mail Gra, 5 AG Orders, 10
Individual, 2 CG USARV, 2 HQDA,
(DAAG-ASO-O) Wash DC 20315, 2 HQDA
(DA-PO-OPD-WOAVN) Wash DC 20315

Brandywine read the orders and then looked up at the General and smiled.

"Colonel Cleaver," General Redling said. "Would you read the citation, please?"

"I would be honored to, General," Cleaver said. "Attention to orders."

Brandywine came to attention.

"Citation," Cleaver began. "CW3 Walter W. Brandywine, W2123490, distinguished himself by heroism while participating in aerial flight, evidenced by voluntary action above and beyond the call of duty. CW3 Brandywine, on 14 April, 1970, was participating as a recovery officer in an aerial assault by the Eleventh ARVN Division. The action was taking place near the village of Memot, Cambodia, during an authorized Cambodian incursion.

"A total of eight aircraft were brought down by enemy fire during the ensuing action, and CW3 Brandywine's helicopter went immediately to work. It was required to make several low passes at low airspeed across enemy held terrain, providing air cover for the crews and infantrymen who were already on the ground.

"CW3 Brandywine flew back and forth across the LZ, exposing himself to intensive, automatic weapons fire from the enemy and allowing his door gunners to engage and mark the positions with smoke. This enabled the gunships to come up and conduct air strikes, eventually eliminating the enemy positions.

"CW3 Brandywine's actions were in keeping with the highest traditions of the military service and reflect great credit to himself and the United States Army." General Redling then pinned the Distinguished Flying Cross to Brandywine's shirt and stepped back. Brandywine saluted him, and Redling returned the salute. Then, smiling, Redling stuck his hand out. "Congratulations," he said.

"Thank you, General."

"Congratulations," Cleaver said, though it was obvious that his heart was not in the offer.

"Thank you, Colonel," Brandywine said.

"Oh, and I wonder if you would mind signing my book," General Redling said, picking up a copy of *Brandywine's War* from his desk.

"I'd be honored to," Brandywine said. As he autographed the book, he didn't notice General Redling motioning for all the others to leave. Finished with the autograph, he handed the book back to the general. "Well, sir, I'd better get back to my . . ."

"Wait," General Redling said.

Brandywine paused, puzzled by the request, and by the rather strange expression on the General's face. The general picked up a letter from his desk.

"How many years of active duty do you have, Mister Brandywine?"

"Almost eighteen, sir."

"Almost? But not eighteen?"

"I have seventeen years and ten months. I'll have eighteen years in two more months," Brandywine said.

The general shook his head. "In two more months, you would have been safe."

"Safe?"

"From the RIF."

Brandywine felt a hollowness in the pit of his stomach. He knew about the reductions in force. Several of his friends had received their notifications. But these were generally officers who had served much less time than he had.

"I've been riffed?" he asked in a quiet voice.

"Believe me, Mister Brandywine, in light of the award you just received, and your courageous service to our nation, I wish there was some way I could avoid this." Sighing, the general handed Brandywine the letter. "You have thirty days," he said. "Then you will be officially relieved from active duty."

Stunned by this sudden and totally unexpected turn of events, Brandywine left the general's office. He was still looking at the letter as he reached his car.

"Do you want to know why?"

Looking around, Brandywine saw Colonel Cleaver standing by his car, leaning back against it, his arms folded across his chest.

"Yes," Brandywine said. "I want to know why."

"Read the last paragraph in the letter."

Brandywine looked at the letter, then skipped, quickly, down to the last paragraph.

"A complaint has been filed by Colonel Emile L. Cleaver, TC, that you caused to be published a book, without first obtaining clearance from the Department of Army Book and Manuscript Section of the Public Information Office. Upon further investigation, Colonel Cleaver's complaint was substantiated. In addition, the book in question, *Brandywine's War,* is an iconoclastic novel that reflects great discredit to the United States Army Aviation effort in Vietnam and to the United States Army in general.

"Accordingly, your active duty status is revoked, as of thirty days after the date of this notification. The United States Army thanks you for your service to your country."

Brandywine looked up at Cleaver. "You did this?"

"Yes."

"Why?"

The Army was all a game to you, Brandywine," Cleaver said. "For your entire career, you made it a point to show how little you thought of rules and regulations."

"But, that's not true, Colonel," Brandywine said. "I accomplished every mission that was ever given me. My OER's were maximum from day one. I may have pushed the envelope a little in order to get things done, but I never violated a regulation. Not once."

"You are not a conformer, Mister Brandywine," Cleaver said. "You are what some may call a free spirit, but what I would call a loose cannon on the deck. There is simply no place for you in my Army."

"Funny, Colonel," Brandywine said. "And here, all this time, I thought it was the United States Army."

W.W. Brandywine was living in a rented townhouse in downtown Newport News, Virginia. He had been out of the Army for nearly a year, before he was finally able to grasp the fact that he was a civilian. Often he would realize that it was already o nine hundred-he still referred to time by the military clock and dated his checks backwards--and he would feel a sudden sense of panic, as if he were AWOL for not being on duty.

Oddly, it was even stronger when he was sleeping because night after night, in his dreams, he was back on duty. And though he had seen more than his share of death and killing, the dreams were not the kind of war-trauma dreams some veterans experienced. These dreams were mundane day to day, doing his job, kind of dreams.

There was, however, one recurring dream that did haunt him. At least once a week, he would find himself wondering around in the back areas of some military post. He had no idea what post he was on and no idea where he was supposed to be. He knew only that he had to be somewhere, that someone was expecting him, depending on him, but he was lost.

Although the dreams continued, he was gradually coming to grips with his civilian status during his waking hours. This was helped in part because his once, very-short, military-cut hair was now worn long. He also had a full beard. There was very little about his appearance now that suggested he had once been an officer in the United States Army.

His early out had denied him any retirement benefits, but publishing his second novel, *Heart of Nashville*, may have made that less of a problem. Although this book, a novel about the country music scene, was not selling as well as *Brandywine's War* had sold, it was enjoying brisk enough sales to cause his publisher to want another book from him. It also proved to Brandywine that he did not have to write only those stories that he had personally lived; he could write stories about any subject that interested him. And if he worked hard enough at it, he knew he could make a living doing something he loved almost as much as he had loved the Army.

But despite this gradual adaptation to his new status, there was still something missing in his life. He couldn't quite put his finger on what it was, but whatever it was, it left a hole. Maybe it was the camaraderie he had experienced in the Army or the sense of adventure or even the excitement of travel.

He was thinking about leaving Newport News. After all, there was nothing holding him here any longer, not Fort Eustis and certainly not Glenda. He had seen her only once since returning from Vietnam.

Maybe he would move to New York. He had been there two or three times since he got out of the Army, and he had always found it exciting. Besides, that is where the really successful writers lived, wasn't it?

But he didn't really want to move to New York. So far, every visit had been an upbeat experience for him. But if he lived there, every day couldn't be that exciting. He wanted to keep New York, always, as a magic city.

Maybe he would move to Florida; he had always

liked the beach. To him, one of the most disappointing things about Newport News was that it had twenty-three miles of coastline, but only one hundred yards of beach. There was another thing about Newport News that depressed him. As long as he was here, it would always remind him of his two greatest failures: a failed marriage and a failed career.

Brandywine's musings were interrupted by a knock, and thinking it was the pizza he had ordered earlier, he got the money and hurried to open the door.

He was met by a young woman, with straight blonde hair with a flowered headband. On her long shapeless dress were two buttons: one was the peace symbol, the other the slogan *War is unhealthy for children and other living things.*

The young woman laughed. "Why, W, I know I've bleached my hair and let it grow long, but don't you recognize me."

"Jane!" Brandywine said, gathering her into a great, bear-like hug and pulling her to him. He held her as if making a desperate grab to hang on to what once had been his life. Finally, he let her go, and leaning back he looked at her. "You have no idea how beautiful you are to me at this moment," he said. "My God, you are like a cool drink of water in the middle of a desert. What are you doing here?"

"How long will it take you to get packed?" Jane asked.

Brandywine smiled. "Not long," he answered. "Look out front."

Looking into the parking lot of the townhouse complex, he saw a white Dodge van, decorated with rainbows, peace symbols, butterflies, birds, and flowers.

"That's my van," she said.

Brandywine laughed.

Jane had been holding something behind her back. She brought out a garland of daisies and put it on his head.

"Now, you have flowers in your hair," she said. "Let's go to San Francisco."

Order Form

Order *Brandywine's War: Back in Country*--available from:
Skyward Publishing
813 Michael Street
Kennett, MO 63857
info@skywardpublishing.com
573-888-5026

The purchase price is $19.95 per copy and may be made by check or
credit card. Provide your name, street address, city, state, zip code,
email, and phone number.
Add $2.00 for shipping. If a different shipping address, also include
the name, address, city, state, and zip code of the shipping address.

For credit card orders, indicate Visa, Master Card, or Discover. Include
the following:
Card number_____
Three digit security code on back of card_____
Expiration date_____
Name on card_____
Address of cardholder:_____
_____
Phone number_____
Email_____

Shipping Address:
Name_____
Street address_____
City_____
State_____
Zip code_____

We welcome your comments. Please contact the
author at info@skywardpublishing.com.

For bulk orders with discounts, please email
info@skywardpublishing.com